Just Grace and the
Trouble with Cupcakes

Just Grace and the Trouble with Cupcakes

Written and illustrated
by

Charise Mericle Harper

HOUGHTON MIFFLIN HARCOURT
Boston   New York

www.hmhco.com

The text of this book is set in Dante MT.
The illustrations are pen-and-ink drawings digitally colored in Photoshop.

Recipes on pages 189–92 reprinted with permission from *Hello, Cupcake!:
Irresistibly Playful Creations Anyone Can Make* by Karen Tack and
Alan Richardson (Houghton Mifflin Harcourt, 2008).

The Library of Congress has cataloged the hardcover edition as follows:
Harper, Charise Mericle.
Just Grace and the trouble with cupcakes / written and illustrated by Charise
Mericle Harper.
p. cm
Summary: Count on third-grader Grace to cook up a creative compromise
just in time to save the day at the cupcake-themed school fair.
[1. Cupcakes—Fiction. 2. Fairs—Fiction. 3. Schools—Fiction.] I. Title.
PZ7.H231323Jum 2013
[Fic]—dc23
2012033824
ISBN: 978-0-547-87744-0 hardcover
ISBN: 978-0-544-33910-1 paperback

Manufactured in the United States of America
DOC 10 9 8 7 6 5 4 3 2
4500542520

This book is for all cupcake lovers,
especially the two who live right here
in the house with me.

SIX THINGS YOU CANNOT TELL JUST BY LOOKING AT ME

1. That some people think my name is Just Grace, even though it's only Grace. This is the kind of thing can happen if your teacher doesn't listen properly when you say, "I want you to call me just Grace."

2. That I am super lucky because I have Mimi, my best friend in the whole world, living right next door to me. And even better than that: our bedroom windows are right across from each other.

ME WAVING AT MIMI FROM MY WINDOW

MIMI WAVING AT ME FROM HER WINDOW

3. That I have a friend named Augustine Dupre who is a French flight attendant, and
   she lives with her husband in a cool apart-
   ment that is right in the basement of my
   very own house.

4. That I like to draw comics because they
   make me happy.

5. That I am in third grade, and that my teacher is Miss Lois.

6. That I have a girl dog and her name is Mr. Scruffers. She came with that name so I couldn't change it, but it's okay, because now I am used to it.

THE BEST THING ABOUT BEING IN MISS LOIS'S CLASS

Everyone in our whole class has been waiting for the day when Miss Lois says, "Today we are going to start working on the spring fair." And that is because every year Miss

Lois's class does a special spring fair project. It's the most fun thing you get to do in her class, and the only reason why when other people find out you have Miss Lois as a teacher they say, "You're so lucky."

THE FIVE THINGS I KNOW ABOUT
THE SPRING FAIR

1. It's exciting, fun, and there are games and prizes and even giant blow-up rides.
2. Everyone comes—even people who are not in our school.
3. Our class gets to make up games and work at the fair.
4. Everyone helps at the fair, even moms and dads.
5. There is a cotton candy machine.

Every Monday since spring started I have been thinking, *I bet today's the day we get to start on the fair.* And every Monday I have been 100 percent wrong!

HOW I KNOW THAT MISS LOIS WILL TALK ABOUT THE FAIR ON A MONDAY

When Miss Lois tells her class it's time to work on the spring fair, she always does it in exactly the same way. I know this because Grace F.'s cousin Benny had Miss Lois for a teacher last year, and he told Grace F. all about it.

RIGHT AFTER THE MONDAY ANNOUNCEMENTS MISS LOIS WENT TO THE CLOSET, AND WHEN SHE CAME BACK OUT SHE WAS WEARING HER BIG CRAZY HAT FROM LAST YEAR'S FAIR.

Benny said that as soon as everyone saw the hat they started clapping and shouting like crazy, and that Miss Lois just stood at the front of the class smiling and nodding. This part of the story is hard to believe, because Miss Lois is not the kind of teacher who is okay with shouting. The part that I do believe is when Benny said it was super fun. Kids don't lie about fun.

If you looked at Miss Lois, you would never think that she is the kind of person who would wear a crazy hat. That's why just looking at people can fool you about what they are really like on the inside. Miss Lois is full of other surprises, too, because she doesn't just wear crazy hats—she makes them, too! And all by herself!

Mimi says Miss Lois should get the gold star of making giant crazy hats, because her hats are excellent and very creative. That's a big compliment, because Mimi knows a lot about crafts, and she wouldn't give Miss Lois a gold star unless she deserved it.

THE THING I HAVE BEEN WAITING TO SEE

MISS LOIS'S SURPRISE

I couldn't believe it! The surprise happened today! And it wasn't even Monday—it was Friday.

Fifteen minutes before class ended, Miss Lois came out from the closet wearing her giant nest hat from last year. Instantly everyone knew what that meant—it was time to work on the spring fair.

WHAT I LEARNED ABOUT GRACE'S COUSIN

Benny is an exaggerator, because as soon as Robert Walters started shouting, Miss Lois pointed her finger at him and said, "Robert! No shouting." She did let us clap, though, so that part was true.

WHAT IS NOT EASY

When we were walking home, Mimi could

tell that I was a little bit unhappy. Best friends are like that—they can tell about your inside feelings even if your outsides look totally normal. I told her I was grumpy about Miss Lois doing the Spring Fair announcement on a Friday.

WHAT MIMI SAID ABOUT MISS LOIS

"Maybe she was too excited to wait until Monday." "I know," I said. "But still, I wish it hadn't happened today. Grandma is coming tomorrow, and now my brain is going to be confused about which fun thing to think about." "I think your brain can think of more than one thing at once," said Mimi. I looked at her and nodded. I felt better than before. Now I was mostly happy and only a tiny bit grumpy.

GRUMPY + HAPPY = GRAPPY

It was a brand-new feeling word. "There should be more words for feelings," I said. Mimi nodded and right then I decided to keep a list.

"What are you going to do with your grandma?" asked Mimi. It was a good question, and it stopped me from thinking about feelings, which was also good. I needed my thinking energy to be on Grandma, because I had a big plan, and it was to make her visit 100 percent perfect.

I told Mimi about the special dinner Mom was making, the surprise fancy brunch we were taking Grandma to, and the big sign I was going to put up right over Grandma's door.

But the thing I was excited about more than anything else was that Grandma was finally going to meet Mr. Scruffers. I couldn't believe it hadn't happened yet. Grandma had seen lots of pictures of Mr. Scruffers, but this was the first time she was going to meet her—person to dog.

"Your grandma is going to love Mr. Scruffers!" said Mimi. "She's the best dog ever!" It was really nice to hear Mimi say that. It made me feel good, plus I knew it was true. "I've been teaching Mr. Scruffers a new trick," I said. "Grandma loves dogs that do tricks." Mimi looked surprised. "A new trick? Can she do it yet?" she asked. I was going to tell her about it, but then suddenly I had a better idea.

MY BETTER IDEA

Mimi and I were standing out on the path to my front door, so I grabbed her hand and pulled her toward it. "Come in," I said. "I'll show you." Mr. Scruffers was on the other side of the door, barking like crazy. Mimi took a step back. She doesn't like it when Mr. Scruffers is super excited and jumpy.

Mimi turned around. "What if I go home and drop off my backpack?" she asked. "Then I'll come back." "Okay," I said. I watched her go, and then slowly I opened the door, ready to face the flying furball of energy.

WHAT FEELS REALLY GREAT

Having a dog be super excited to see you. Mr. Scruffers always acts like I've been away forever, even if I've only been gone for five minutes. Dogs are special that way. They are filled with love. Even though I really like cats, they are not the same as dogs. Crinkles is the cat next door, and even though he really likes me and we have been friends for a long time, he still does not have the same kind of love as Mr. Scruffers does.

I'M NOT EXCITED TO SEE YOU. I JUST SAW YOU YESTERDAY.

The best way to get Mr. Scruffers to calm down fast is to take her outside to the backyard. She loves sniffing around for squirrels. It's too bad you can't arrange a special squirrel-chasing surprise. That would be a perfect dog present.

THIS IS SO EXCITING.

OK, YOU REMEMBER WHAT TO DO, RIGHT?

AS SOON AS THE DOG COMES OUT I TWITCH MY TAIL AND THEN RUN.

MR. SCRUFFERS'S NEW TRICK

I thought the new trick would be easy for Mr. Scruffers to learn, because she already knew all the parts of it. But I was wrong. Even with a whole box of dog treats, the new trick was not easy.

THE PARTS MR. SCRUFFERS KNOWS HOW TO DO

WHAT THE NEW TRICK IS SUPPOSED TO LOOK LIKE

Mr. Scruffers was good at the sitting part, but every time I grabbed her paw she fell over onto the ground. If she could talk, she probably would have said, "What is it with you and the paw? Can I please just have it back, and can you give me that cookie you're holding?" It's not easy to say "No cookie" when your dog is at least trying. It doesn't seem fair. So even though Mr. Scruffers got the trick wrong, I gave her the treat. It's too bad that falling down wasn't an impressive trick, because she was really good at that part.

I was standing there watching her when all of a sudden she jumped up and ran to the back door. I looked up and there was Mimi. "Did she do it?" asked Mimi. I shook my head. "I think it's hopeless," I said. "She doesn't get what she's supposed to do." I explained the trick to Mimi, and told her how it was supposed to work. "It's not like it's an impossible trick," I complained. I didn't say it out loud, but a big part of me was feeling like giving up.

AN IMPOSSIBLE TRICK

HOW MIMI CHANGED EVERYTHING

"Let me help," said Mimi. "I'll hold the cookie and you can show her what to do." I thought for a moment and then said, "Okay." It wasn't how I would normally teach a trick, but maybe Mimi was right. It was worth a try.

I called Mr. Scruffers over and made her sit next to me, and then I told Mimi where to hold the cookie. "Watch me," I said, and then I showed Mr. Scruffers what to do.

As soon as I put my hand out Mimi burst out laughing. She was laughing so hard, she dropped the cookie. Of course Mr. Scruffers jumped up and ate it. "I didn't mean for you to do the trick," laughed Mimi. "I thought you'd hold up Mr. Scruffers's paw and show her that way." Suddenly I was laughing too.

Teaching Mr. Scruffers a trick with Mimi was definitely more fun than doing it by myself.

After we stopped laughing, we decided to try the trick Mimi's way. Mimi is good at training. She isn't an expert with dogs, but she's an expert with little brothers, and that's probably not much different. Robert is Mimi's little brother, and she's trained him to do—and not do—a whole bunch of things. Because of Mimi he knows not to throw balls in the street, not to flush socks down the toilet, and to always throw a lollipop in the garbage if it falls out of your mouth onto the sidewalk. Suddenly I was filled with training energy. Plus, Mr. Scruffers's trick seemed a whole lot easier to teach than those other things.

"I'll get more treats!" I said. I ran into the house and grabbed the whole box of cookies. When I got back outside Mimi was kicking Mr. Scruffers's ball for her. Chasing a ball is Mr. Scruffers's third favorite game in the whole world. It comes right after chasing squirrels and chasing Crinkles. The only bad thing about the ball game is that once you start it, Mr. Scruffers doesn't ever want you to stop. I wasn't so sure she was going to be interested in cookies and learning a new trick when her brain was thinking about chasing the ball. I was hoping she was like me. Maybe she could think about two things at once.

THE SAD BUT TRUE THING

Mr. Scruffers has a one-thing-at-a-time-only kind of brain. When I shook the box of cookies, she looked up at me for a second but then went right back to staring at the ball beside Mimi's foot.

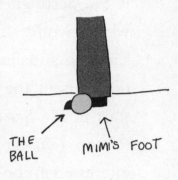

THE BALL

MIMI'S FOOT

"I think we're going to have to use the ball instead of the cookies," I said. Mimi pulled her foot back and gave it a little kick. It was a bad kick, but Mr. Scruffers didn't care. She pounced on the ball and then held it in her mouth, biting and slobbering all over it.

"I'm not touching that!" said Mimi. She moved away. "It's covered with slobber." Mimi rubbed her hands against her pants, like just talking about it had made them slimy. I couldn't blame her—it was pretty disgusting, but I was used to it, and I loved Mr. Scruffers, so it was different for me. "That's okay," I said. "I'll hold the ball. You can hold Mr. Scruffers." "Okay," said Mimi. "I'll try."

WHAT WAS EASY TO DO

Hold up Mr. Scruffers.

WHAT WAS IMPOSSIBLE TO DO

Have Mr. Scruffers stay up once you let go. Every time Mimi grabbed her paw, she fell over. Mr. Scruffers watched us watching her. I shook my head. It was not a trick.

WHAT WAS TOO BAD

That Mr. Scruffers couldn't understand what we wanted her to do. Out of all the words I said, Mr. Scruffers probably didn't understand any of them.

I tried saying "Good dog" a lot, but that didn't help either. After the sixth time of trying the trick, instead of coming back to me, she ran up the steps and scratched her paw against the door. She wanted to go in. That pretty much made it official. She hated the trick. I looked at Mimi and shook my head. There was no way it was going to work.

Mimi tried to make me feel better. "Maybe we could make Mr. Scruffers look special. I could help you make a bow for her." This was a nice thing for Mimi to do. I nodded and gave her a mini smile. It's not easy to be happy when your big plan for something you really wanted has just failed.

In the end we let Mr. Scruffers back inside and went over to Mimi's house. Making a bow was going to be a lot easier than teaching Mr. Scruffers a new trick. I just hoped it was going to work as good as a trick would have.

WHAT I REALLY WANTED TO HAPPEN

GRANDMA

MIMI'S HOUSE

Mimi has a ton of craft supplies, but it took me only about two seconds to pick out the exact perfect thing to use for Mr. Scruffers's bow. Grandma's favorite colors are yellow and blue, and right there in the middle of everything was some yellow and blue polka-dot fabric. "Perfect," said Mimi. "All we have to do is cut out the parts for the bow and then sew it up." Mimi is excellent at making things, so I let her do the cutting and sewing part. While she did that, I cleaned up the huge pile of stuff she had pulled out of her closet. Mimi is also excellent at making a mess.

MIMI SURE KNOWS HOW TO MAKE A BIG MESS.

Now that I didn't have to think about Grandma anymore, I started thinking about the spring fair. The first thing our class had to do was come up with a theme for our part of the fair. Last year's class picked birds, so all their games were bird-themed—that's why Miss Lois's hat was a giant nest.

Miss Lois says she doesn't want a hundred theme ideas, so each person is only allowed to suggest one idea. Once all the ideas are together, we're going to vote on one to be our class theme. Voting on stuff never makes everybody happy, so Miss Lois is going to have to be ready for one very happy winner and a lot of other people being sad.

WHAT IS NOT EASY

Just because you want to think of a good idea doesn't mean you can.

Not being able to think of anything good was making me feel frustrated, and not just frustrated, but mad and frustrated. I was mustrated. "Mustrated!" I said it out loud. Mimi looked up. "What's that?" she asked. "A mustard?" I shook my head. "No, it's mad plus frustrated," I shook my head and made a grumpy face. "You're good at those put-together words," said Mimi. I smiled. Compliments always feel good. They are like being rained on by happiness.

About an hour later we had a new bow for Mr. Scruffers and a list of two pretty good fair ideas.

OUR FAIR IDEAS AND WHO THOUGHT OF THEM

1. SUPERPOWERS (There would be games about different superpowers.) Me

2. CANDY (Every game could have something to do with a different kind of candy.) Mimi

Once you have an idea you really like it's hard to think of anything else that seems better. I was happy with my superpowers idea. It fit me.

WHAT I COULD TELL RIGHT AWAY

Candy was the best idea on the list. Best and favorite are not the same thing. My idea was still my favorite, but I knew candy was the kind of idea our whole class was going to go crazy for.

I'M THE BEST IDEA! EVERYONE ♥S CANDY!

THE PROMISE

I looked at Mimi and said, "If everyone likes your idea the best, I'm not going to try to make my idea be the winner. I don't want our ideas to fight against each other." Mimi looked surprised. "That's another good idea," she said, and she smiled. "I don't want that either. If your idea is the most popular, I won't say another word about my idea." "Pinky swear," I said, and I held out my pinky. "Pinky swear," said Mimi, and we made it official.

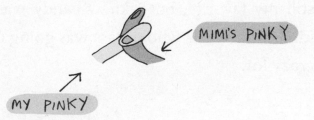

MIMI'S PINKY

MY PINKY

After the pinky swear, Mimi came back to my house so we could try the new bow on Mr. Scruffers. Of course Mr. Scruffers hated it, but that wasn't a surprise—she hates all accessories. At first she tried to bite it off, but as soon as we took her outside and threw the ball, she sort of forgot that she was wearing it. It looked super cute. All I had to do was put it on just before Grandma arrived and then keep Mr. Scruffers from chewing it off until Grandma saw it. How hard could that be?

WHAT MOM SAID ABOUT GRANDMA

She said, "We have to be careful and not tire Grandma out before her big trip." I nodded, but I was sad. I wasn't super happy that Grandma was only staying with us for the weekend. On Sunday night she was flying to France to meet Mr. Costello, her boyfriend, and some of her other friends from Shady Grove—that's the place where she lives. They were all going on an amazing trip, to visit French castles and the city of Paris. It sounded fantastic, and a lot better than two weeks in school.

Whenever Grandma and I see each other, we always try to have special time that's just the two of us. I made sure to remind Mom about that so she wouldn't forget. After I asked her about a hundred times, Mom finally gave me two choices—lunch tomorrow or two hours in the afternoon on Sunday. I picked lunch, because it was perfect for my plan, and that plan started with a "p" and ended with a "c."

MY PICNIC PLAN

1. Put the bow on Mr. Scruffers and take Grandma and Mr. Scruffers on a picnic.

2. Sit on the swinging bench at the park with Grandma and Mr. Scruffers.

MAP OF THE PARK

3. Eat delicious sandwiches and have iced tea mixed with lemonade as a drink.

FUN-SHAPED SANDWICHES CUT OUT WITH MOM'S COOKIE CUTTERS

ICED-T WITH

MY FAVORITE DRINK IN A BOX

4. Visit with Grandma and take a photo of me, Grandma, and Mr. Scruffers all together, so I can remember the day and keep it forever.

Mom said she would help out by making snickerdoodle cookies. I love Mom's snickerdoodle cookies. I would almost pick them over cotton candy, but I didn't tell her that. That's not a good thing to tell a mom. That kind of thing could turn out bad later.

After Mom left for the store I went upstairs to start on the sign for Grandma. She is staying in the room next to me. It's nice to have her close. When Mimi's grandmother visits she has to stay in their basement. I wouldn't like that. I like having my family right around me.

While I was making the Welcome sign, I had a new idea of something else to do. It was almost even better than the sign.

It was good that Mom was gone a long time, because getting everything done took longer than I thought it would. When she finally got back, I was starving for dinner and almost finished.

AFTER DINNER

When all the dishes were done, Mom and Dad helped me put up the sign I'd made for Grandma. They loved it. Grandma's not famous, but I felt like she almost could be, because that's how excited I was to see her.

WELCOME

I CAN'T BELIEVE SHE'S ALMOST HERE.

DOOR TO GRANDMA'S ROOM

FEELINGS OF EXCITEMENT

I told Mr. Scruffers all about Grandma, and even though she couldn't understand what I was saying, she was a good listener. I couldn't wait for them to meet. It was going to be love at first sight.

THE NEXT MORNING

Mr. Scruffers and I were up early. The sun was shining, and it was a perfect day for a picnic. Mom must have been excited about Grandma too, because she was up before we were, and she never gets up that early. She offered to make me French toast. I like to have French toast when I need extra energy, or if am worried about something, but today even though I was neither of those things, I still said yes. Having extra energy is never a bad thing.

THE THING THAT MADE ME EXTRA HAPPY

Seeing a plate of fresh snickerdoodles on the counter. Mom said not to eat any because we were saving them for Grandma.

YUMMY SNICKERDOODLE COOKIES

WHAT IS HARD TO DO

Not take a cookie just to see if it tastes as good as it smells.

WAITING FOR GRANDMA

After breakfast Dad told me to take Mr. Scruffers outside and play with her. "Throw the ball and tire her out," he said. Mr. Scruffers heard Dad say "ball" and "outside," so she was looking at me with her ears up. When she hears words she understands, she gets super interested and watches to see what's going to happen next. As soon as I said "Okay," and stood up, Mr. Scruffers ran to the back door. She's smart about the words she knows.

Using up some of her energy before Grandma got here was a good idea. Even though Grandma loves dogs, she was probably like Mimi. Not everyone likes jumping, barking dogs, and Barnaby, Grandma's old dog, definitely didn't do either of those things.

I played ball with Mr. Scruffers for almost an hour. It was a new record. At the end Mr. Scruffers was really tired and my arm was sore. It was a workout for both of us.

The rest of the morning took forever to go by. Waiting time moves a lot slower than regular time. The only fun thing I did after playing with Mr. Scruffers was to get the picnic ready. Mom helped me make the sand-wiches, but everything else I did by myself. When I was done I set it out on the counter, just to be sure there was nothing missing. It looked perfect.

THE AIRPORT

Normally when Grandma comes, I go with Mom to the airport to get her, but this time was different. This time I was staying home. It felt weird to see Mom drive off without me, but I didn't have a choice. I wanted Mr. Scruffers to be wearing her new bow when

Grandma met her, and there was no way I could put the bow on her and then leave the house. I knew Mr. Scruffers—the minute I was gone she'd rip it off.

MR. SCRUFFERS LYING

I'LL KEEP THIS BOW ON. I PROMISE!

TOES ON PAW ARE CROSSED

Mr. Scruffers watched out the window with me until Mom's car disappeared, and then we flopped down on the sofa. "Grandma's going to be sad when I'm not at the airport," I said. Mr. Scruffers didn't look up. "I don't want you to feel bad, but it's all because of you." She didn't move. I petted her head. "That's okay. You're worth it." We sat there for a long time—me talking and her listening. I made sure not to use even one of her jump-up-and-get-excited words, so it was pretty relaxing.

MR. SCRUFFERS'S JUMP-UP-AND-GET-EXCITED WORDS

Squirrel

Treat

Cookie

Cat

Walk

Ball

Outside

Park

After about thirty minutes, I went up to my room to get the bow so I could be ready. Of course, Mr. Scruffers followed me. As soon as she saw the bow, she put her tail down and looked up at me with sad eyes. That's how much she hated it. "It'll be okay," I said. "You only have to wear it for five minutes." She didn't look any happier. I put the bow around my neck like a scarf and tied it up. "See! It's not that bad." I got on the bed and bounced up and down so she could see how happy it made me. Suddenly she was better. Mr. Scruffers loves jumping games.

SEE, MR. SCRUFFERS. IT'S FUN!

ME JUMPING ON THE BED.

Jumping on the bed probably wasn't the best thing to do right before Grandma was coming, but I didn't think about that. All I was thinking about was trying to make Mr. Scruffers happy.

WHAT DID NOT HAPPEN

I didn't hear the front door open, but Mr. Scruffers did. She has ears like a superhero. One second she was jumping on the bed with me, and the next second she was gone—racing down the stairs barking her head off.

Instantly I knew, *This is not good.* I ran after her, but she is fast. I couldn't catch her to put on her bow.

THE POWER OF TEA AND COOKIES

Tea and cookies can make you feel better, especially if you are disappointed about not having your dog look fancy to meet your grandma. Grandma didn't mind, though— she liked Mr. Scruffers right away.

Grandma brought me a present. Usually I rip the paper, but with Grandma and Mom watching I was more careful than normal. After I got the paper off there was still more unwrapping.

PRESENT WRAPPED IN BUBBLEWRAP.

WHAT YOUR BRAIN THINKS WHEN YOU SEE BUBBLEWRAP

YAY! I CAN'T WAIT TO POP THOSE BUBBLES.

The bubble wrap was easy to get off, and inside in the middle of it all was a beautiful little pot with a lid. It was my favorite colors, blue and green. I shook it—there was something inside. "It's a lucky penny pot," said Grandma. "And there are two lucky pennies inside. Every time you find a lucky penny, you can put it in your pot, and every time you need a lucky penny, you can take one out." Then Grandma whispered, "Sometimes it's a good idea to save a lucky penny for a day when you'll really need it."

I WISH GRANDMA'S VISIT IS PERFECT.

MR. SCRUFFERS'S BOW, WHICH WAS GETTING ITCHY ON MY NECK.

THE LUCKY PENNY POT

"Thank you," I said. I leaned over and gave Grandma a hug. I already had a wish, but I didn't say anything. Wishes are the kind of things you keep secret, especially if you want them to come true.

While Mom and Grandma were making tea, I snuck one of the pennies out of the pot and made my wish. I'd already messed up the bow, and I didn't want anything else to go wrong. Grandma hadn't said what to do with pennies after you used them, so I just put it in my pocket. I'd have to ask about that later. When we all sat down it was like a real tea party. Mom even made a special tea for me. At first I didn't like it very much, but after Mom put maple syrup in it, I loved it. I took a cookie and listened to Grandma talk about her trip. Listening to her made me wish I had two more pennies. Wishes were a lot easier to think of than theme ideas.

MY TWO NEW WISHES
1. That I could see the Eiffel Tower,

because it is the most famous thing about France.

2. That Grandma and I could get the good bench at the park.

LATER IN THE MORNING

Mom thought I forgot about the picnic, but of course I didn't. I was just waiting for the right time to tell Grandma about it. As soon as I told her she was super excited. She loves picnics.

After the picnic was ready I tried to put Mr. Scruffers's bow around her neck, but she backed away and ran behind the sofa. "Oh, she doesn't like it," said Grandma. "Why don't you put it on the picnic bag instead. It'll look pretty there." For a second I thought about saying, *No, Mr. Scruffers has to wear her bow,* but then I changed my mind. The bow was really for Grandma, and if she wanted to see it on the picnic bag instead of Mr. Scruffers's neck, then that was the place to put it. Mr. Scruffers was probably thinking some nice thoughts about what was happening.

THAT GRANDMA PERSON HAS REALLY GOOD IDEAS!

THE PICNIC

I crossed my fingers the whole way to the park. The best benches are the swinging ones and there are only two of them in the whole park. If somebody was already sitting on them, we'd have to sit on the boring regular benches, and that was not part of my plan.

The best swing bench is the one next to the flower garden and the pond. The other one doesn't have a very good view, just a bunch of bushes, but it's better than nothing. As soon as we got to the park, I saw that two ladies were already sitting on the good bench. I wanted to wait until they got off, but Grandma said, "Look—we're lucky. We can have the other swinging bench." Grandma is good at not getting upset about things. There was a little puddle under the bench, but we got on without getting our feet wet, and once we were swinging, I didn't even notice it anymore.

Mr. Scruffers wanted to sit on the bench with us. I wasn't sure if I should let her, but Grandma said, "The more the merrier," so I let her jump up.

At home no one is allowed to feed Mr. Scruffers from the table. But this was not home, and we were on a bench, not at a table, so I didn't say anything when Grandma gave Mr. Scruffers a piece of her sandwich. It was hard not to share—Mr. Scruffers was watching every single bite we took. At first everything was okay, but then after a few minutes Mr. Scruffers wanted more. When

Mr. Scruffers wants something, she is not quiet. She barks. It was not a relaxing way to eat.

It made me think about Dad's rule.

Dad was right. I could see it happening. We told Mr. Scruffers to stop barking, but that didn't work. All she cared about was Grandma's sandwich, and she wanted that sandwich in her mouth. "I'm sorry," I shouted. It was hard for Grandma to hear me over the barking. "It's my fault," shouted Grandma. I nodded—she was right about that. Suddenly I had an idea. Mr. Scruffers always stops barking when I hold up a ball. I looked in the picnic bag and pulled out an orange. "Look! Ball," I shouted. Mr. Scruffers stopped barking and looked up at the orange. Her tail started to wag. I waved it in the air and chewed my sandwich as fast as I could. It wasn't the best way to eat, but at least it was quiet.

ME WAVING THE ORANGE TO TRICK MR. SCRUFFERS.

CHEW FAST, GRANDMA. THIS ISN'T GOING TO WORK FOR VERY LONG.

I was right about it not working for very long, because after a few more seconds, Mr. Scruffers started to bark at me to throw the ball. To make it more exciting for her I pulled my arm back and pretended like I was going to throw the orange—only by accident, I dropped it. The second the orange left my hand, Mr. Scruffers jumped off the bench to get it. She bumped the picnic bag and knocked the whole thing over, right into the middle of the puddle. It was a disaster!

WHAT GRANDMA SAID

"Oh, Grace, I'm so sorry. I should have said

no to having Mr. Scruffers on the bench."
Having Grandma say that did not make me
feel better. For some reason it did the oppo-
site—suddenly I felt even worse. I tried not
to, but I couldn't help it—I started to cry.

WHAT IS REALLY HARD TO DO

See where you are going when your eyes are
full of tears. I jumped off the bench and landed with both feet right on top of the picnic
bag. Now everything was wet and muddy.
Grandma pulled the bag out of the puddle.
It was all was squashed and dirty. "The cookies!" I cried. They were my favorite part of
the picnic. "There, there," said Grandma.
"I'm sure there's more at home." I shook my

head. I keep track of stuff like that. There were no more. These were the last ones.

Both Grandma and Mr. Scruffers looked at me with sad eyes. That made me feel a little bit better, and I stopped crying. "I have an idea," said Grandma. "Why don't we go home and make some cupcakes. You like cupcakes, don't you?" I nodded. "Well, I have an amazing cupcake recipe. I'll phone Mr. Costello and have him go down and get it from my kitchen. I promise, these will be the best cupcakes you've ever tasted." I wiped my eyes with my hands. Grandma gave me a tissue. "Will you help make them?" she asked. I nodded. "Okay," said Grandma, "let's get home so we can send your mom to the store."

WALKING HOME

I would not have been a good burglar. Each step I took made a funny squishing sound. I didn't mind how it sounded, but I didn't like how it felt. It was cold and soggy and it made my feet feel like they were big wet fish.

Mr. Scruffers was really good the whole way home. It made me wonder if she felt guilty. Grandma carried the muddy picnic bag and didn't even complain when it touched her pants and made a big dirty mark. She cared more about me than she did about fashion. I was lucky.

On the walk home I told Grandma all about the spring fair. "I wish I could help you with it," she said. I said I wished that too, but it was impossible. "I guess I can't help if I'm all the way in France," said Grandma. I nodded my head and felt sad. She was right about that.

WHAT HAPPENED WHEN WE GOT HOME

I went upstairs to get changed and Grandma called Mr. Costello and then made a whole list of things for Mom to get from the store. I could tell that Mom wasn't excited about going, but Grandma is her mom, so she pretty much had to do it.

WHAT MOM BROUGHT HOME

COLORED DECORATING FROSTING

PINK OVAL BALLS

PURPLE STARS

FROSTING COLORS

JELLY BEANS

RED

GREEN

PINK

PURPLE

FROSTING COLORS

WHITE

BLACK AND WHITE SPRINKLES

ORANGE SPRINKLE

YELLOW SPRINKLES

BLUE SPRINKLES

A fast way to get excited about making cupcakes is to get a lot of really cool things to decorate them with. Grandma and I followed her recipe and made the cupcakes. My favorite part is always cracking the eggs, and I showed her how I could almost do it with one hand. It was fun to mix them up, but what I really couldn't wait for was the decorating part. I couldn't wait to use all the new stuff Mom had bought.

A HARD THING TO DO

It's hard to wait for cupcakes to cook and cool down when you are excited about decorating them. While Grandma and I were waiting, we made the frosting. It was so good. If Grandma hadn't been watching, I would have taken take a big spoonful of it and just stuffed it into my mouth. Instead I only licked the spinner things from the mixer.

THE GOOD THING
ABOUT GRANDMAS

Grandma let me pick three colors to color
the frosting. I picked purple, blue, and light
pink. Mom usually only lets me pick one col-
or, so I was glad that Grandma was in charge.
Sometimes grandparents are more fun than
parents. It's probably because they don't see
you every day. If I weren't around every day,
Mom would probably be nicer too.

WHAT CUPCAKES LOOK LIKE
WITHOUT ICING

WE LOOK LIKE LITTLE BALD MEN.

MY HEAD NEEDS A COVERING.

WHAT CUPCAKES LOOK LIKE
WITH ICING

THE FUN PART

Decorating the cupcakes was just as fun as I thought it would be. Grandma is a pretty good at it, but she said I was better. When we were done, I took photos of all my cupcakes so I could to remember them. They looked almost too good to eat (but I knew I would eat them, so it was a good thing to do). Mom said I was only allowed to have one cupcake or I wouldn't be hungry for dinner, but when she wasn't looking, Grandma winked at me and said, "You can have two."

It was hard to pick which cupcakes to eat first. I decided to save the best ones for last and picked two that were not my favorites. As soon as I took my first bite, I knew that Grandma had been telling the truth. These were the best cupcakes I had ever tasted. I was glad that she said I could have two. To only eat one would have been almost impossible. "These are amazing!" I said. Grandma smiled. "I told you they would be," she said. I was too busy eating to do any more talking, but my brain wasn't too busy to think, and it was thinking something that was a surprise.

I'M GLAD THE PICNIC FELL INTO THE PUDDLE.

Grandma says that sometimes if you are lucky, bad things can turn into good things. Suddenly I was feeling lucky, because this was definitely one of those times.

WHAT MOM WAS RIGHT ABOUT

I wasn't hungry for dinner. It was hard to eat everything Mom put on my plate, even though we were having salmon and mashed potatoes and I like both those things. But I made myself eat everything because I knew if I didn't, Mom would say, "No cupcakes for dessert!" And I had to have another cupcake. Mom is not a big cupcake person, but when she took a bite of Grandma's cupcake, she closed her eyes and said, "MMMMM!" Dad liked them too, but that was no surprise, because he loves anything sweet.

Grandma likes card games, so before bed we played a couple of games of Uno. I was proud of myself. I didn't get one bit upset even though I lost all three games in a row.

When I got to my room, I looked across at Mimi's window to see if she was still up, but she wasn't—her curtains were closed. I really wanted us to flash our lights to each other, but it was too late. When you are used to doing something, not doing it can make you feel a little bit sad. Even though Mimi wasn't watching, I still flashed my lights three times for her. It helped. I felt better.

SUNDAY

Today was the special brunch at the castle. Even though it wasn't a real French castle like the one Grandma was going to see, it was still a castle, and that was pretty exciting. Mom said to wear something nice, so I put on my best dress, the one I'd worn to Augustine Dupre's wedding.

THE CASTLE

It took a while to get to the restaurant, but it was worth it, because as soon as we saw it, we all said, "Oooh!" and "Ahhh!" It looked like a real castle. The inside did not look as much like a castle as the outside. Mom said she was happy about that. She said modern things were more comfortable.

When French toast is on a menu, it's almost impossible for me to order something else. Favorite things are like that—you can't ignore them. It was a good choice because the French toast was excellent. I was glad that Mom didn't ask if it was better than hers, because it was, and I'm not very good at lying.

THE LIE I DIDN'T HAVE TO SAY

After we finished eating, there wasn't much to do, so we went home. Mom said she had been hoping there were gardens to walk through, but there weren't. Mom and Grandma were the only ones disappointed about that, because Dad and I both think that looking at plants is pretty boring.

As soon as we got home I went upstairs and got changed. A fancy dress is not a good choice for playing ball with a dog. Grandma was getting changed too, and she called me to come to her room. "You were sneaky," she said. She held up a bunch of the notes I had made her. "Did I find them all?" she asked. I looked around the room to see if there were any left. The only one she missed was under the bed. "Oh, I'm too old to go crawling under there," said Grandma. "Okay," I said, "next time I'll do them all higher." Saying that made me think about how Grandma was almost leaving, and how I didn't want her to go. "You didn't even see Mimi," I said. "Well, is she home?" asked Grandma. "She could come over now." "Oh, Grandma!" I said. "You're the best!" I gave her a hug and ran to get Mimi.

I'd been dying to see Mimi all morning. I couldn't wait to give her one of the cupcakes we'd made. I raced down the stairs, out the door, and across the lawn to Mimi's house. I was in too much of a rush to do my special knock, so I just rang the bell. A few seconds later Mimi's dad came to the door. That was a bad sign. He only answers the door if Mimi and her mom aren't there.

"I'm sorry, Grace," he said. "Mimi's out with her mom and Robert for the day." "For the whole day?" I asked. "Are you sure?"

Mimi's dad nodded, and then we both just stood there. Finally I said, "Oh. Okay then," and turned around and walked home. It was not what I wanted.

NOW MIMI WON'T SEE GRANDMA.

SAD ME

I didn't want Grandma to know I was sad, so as soon as I got home, I pretended like Mimi not being there was okay. The rest of the day went by super fast. Grandma showed me a map of France, and we found Paris and two of the castles she was going to visit. Even though we'd eaten in a restaurant that looked like a castle, I had a feeling that real castles were probably more exciting. She was so lucky. It doesn't happen very often, but sometimes you can be jealous of a grandma.

I told Grandma that it was too bad we couldn't ask Augustine Dupre for some France tips. "She's away in France for one whole month," I said. "Maybe you'll see her." Grandma laughed and said, "That would be amazing." I didn't want it to, but it made me feel even worse about not going.

GOING TO SAY GOODBYE

This time when Mom went to the airport, I came too. Mom was glad about that—she said it would make her feel better. I didn't say anything, but I wasn't sure how having another sad person in the car was going to be better than being sad all by herself. Grandma's plane was late, so we sat with her while she waited. When Mom went to the bathroom, Grandma said, "Mr. Scruffers is a wonderful dog. Seeing you together makes me a little bit jealous. I wish I had my Barnaby back." Barnaby was Grandma's old dog. He died two years ago. It was sad that she still missed him, but it was a nice compliment for Mr. Scruffers. I could see why Mom got sad at the airport. Unless you were going somewhere or meeting someone, it wasn't a very fun place to be. It's no fun to say goodbye.

WHAT HAPPENED NEXT

Nothing. Mom and I went home, and then it was just me and Mr. Scruffers hanging around for the whole rest of the day. The only fun thing we did was go for a walk around the block, and it wasn't even that fun. Plus we didn't see a single squirrel, and that's her favorite part about walks.

WHAT YOU CAN EAT FOR BREAKFAST IF YOUR MOM IS NOT LOOKING

BREAKFAST CUPCAKE

Cupcakes have special powers. When I started the cupcake I was still a little grumpy from yesterday, but by the time I took the last bite, I felt 100 percent better. I would have had another one, but Mom walked into the kitchen, so I had a banana instead.

HAPPY BANANA

I GOT PICKED INSTEAD OF A CUPCAKE!

BUT ONLY BECAUSE A MOM WAS WATCHING.

WHY I WAS EXCITED TO GO TO SCHOOL

1. So I could tell Mimi all about my visit with Grandma.
2. To find out where she had been all yesterday.
3. So I could give her a cupcake.
4. Because Miss Lois was going to talk about the spring fair.

Mom saw me putting a cupcake in my lunch bag and shook her head. "You already had one of those today," she said. I looked up like I didn't know what she was talking about, but inside I was shocked. How did she know I'd had a cupcake? Sometimes moms have super-

HELP ME! I'M STUCK UNDER THIS GIANT ROCK!!

YOU HAD ORANGE JUICE AND WAFFLES FOR BREAKFAST.

THAT'S TRUE, BUT THAT'S NOT HELPING.

A MOM USING HER SUPERPOWER

powers about food. It's too bad they can't get powers that are more useful.

"It's not for me—it's for Mimi," I said. "Can't I take it to give to her at lunch?" Mom looked at me like she was trying to decide if I was telling the truth or not. Finally she nodded and said, "Okay, but only one."

MIMI'S SURPRISE

Two minutes later Mimi knocked on the door. She was super early, but it didn't matter—I was happy to see her. It was too early to leave for school, so she dropped her backpack at the door and came in. She had a paper bag in her hand and was shaking it front of me. "Look," she said. She shook it again. "I got you something." "Should I guess?" I asked. "You'll never guess," she said. "It's impossible." She handed me the bag. I looked inside. It was some kind of ball.

"It's a superpower guessing ball," said Mimi. "And it's got the real *Unlikely Heroes* logo printed on the side of it." I pulled the ball out of the bag and looked at it. Mimi was right. I couldn't believe it. *Unlikely Heroes* was our favorite show in the whole world, and there right on the side of the ball was the logo for the show. This was a real *Unlikely Heroes* souvenir! My mouth dropped open.

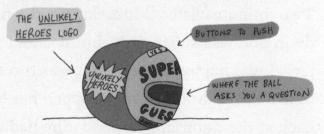

Unlikely Heroes was a show about how regular people or animals used a sudden superpower or skill to save other people from getting hurt. It was hard to believe that such amazing things could happen, but they did. Everything on the show was 100 percent all true!

I smiled at Mimi. It was the best present ever. "Where did you get it?" I asked. "You'll never believe this," said Mimi. "But my mom has a friend named Maureen whose daughter got to work on the show for six weeks last summer, and she got a whole bunch of *Unlikely Heroes* stuff for free. Yesterday we went to visit Maureen and she let us pick a few things out. Robert got a ball that says *Unlikely Heroes,* but this is way better." "Did you just get this one?" I asked. Suddenly I felt weird about taking Mimi's present. "No, don't worry," said Mimi. "I told her my best friend was a huge fan too, so she let me have two of them. I used mine last night, and it really works."

The only bad thing about the present was that I couldn't bring it to school. Miss Lois has a rule about toys at school. I only had time to try it once before we left, but Mimi was right—it really worked!

SUPER SPEED

ME USING THE BALL AND THINKING OF A SUPERPOWER.

HOW THE BALL WORKS

1 YOU THINK OF A SUPERPOWER.

2 THE BALL ASKS YOU QUESTIONS AND YOU POSH THE RIGHT ANSWER BUTTON.

YES NEVER NO
SUPERPOWER
GUESSING BALL
RARELY SOMETIMES ALWAYS

TOP 3 ANSWER BUTTONS.

QUESTION COMES ON THIS SCREEN.

BOTTOM 3 ANSWER BUTTONS.

3 THE BALL ASKS YOU LOTS OF QUESTIONS ABOUT YOUR SUPERPOWER.

4 THE BALL TELLS YOU WHAT SUPERPOWER YOU WERE THINKING ABOUT.

It was hard to stop playing with the ball and go to school, but Mom made it easier by yelling at me that I was going to be late. A yelling mom can really get you moving.

PUT THAT TOY DOWN AND GET TO SCHOOL!

THE TWO GOOD THINGS THAT HAPPENED AT SCHOOL IN THE MORNING

1. We used up a big part of the morning talking about the fair.
2. Owen 1 got sent to the not-paying-attention chair almost as soon as we all sat down. It was nice to have him not sitting behind me, because one of his favorite things to do is poke me in the back with his pencil every two minutes.

At lunchtime I gave Mimi the cupcake I'd brought. She said it was the best cupcake her mouth had ever tasted. "Did you bring any more?" she asked. I shook my head. I knew exactly how she felt. It was hard to eat only one.

MIMI'S MOUTH IS WANTING MORE CUPCAKES

AFTER LUNCH

Miss Lois said the first thing we needed to do was to decide on our theme for the spring fair. She said, "I don't want to do anything I've done before, so I'm going to write down all the ideas that you CANNOT pick." After she said this, she wrote down the ideas her old classes had already done.

MISS LOIS'S FIVE IDEAS THAT WE CAN'T PICK BECAUSE SHE'S DONE THEM BEFORE

Birds
Seasons
Pets
The Beach
Haunted House

WHAT HAPPENED NEXT

Miss Lois said she was ready to hear our

suggestions, and instantly everyone put their hands up. There were a lot of ideas and Miss Lois wrote them all on the board.

Some ideas were good, some were bad, and some were not a surprise. No one was surprised when Marta said "Fairies." She loves fairies, and she and her friends play fairy games every recess. It would have been a surprise if she'd said something else.

HOW BOYS FEEL ABOUT FAIRIES

As the idea list got longer, fewer and fewer people had their hands up. I looked over at Mimi—neither of us had said our ideas yet. She saw me looking at her, and put her hand up and waved it around. When Miss Lois pointed to her Mimi said, "Candy." Instantly everyone was talking. Everyone loves candy. I could tell, candy was definitely going to win. Mimi had a big smile on her face—she was really happy. No one else's idea had gotten everyone so excited.

Suddenly I thought of a new idea, something better than my superpowers idea. It was something people loved maybe even more than candy. Without even thinking about it, I put my hand in the air and shouted out what I was thinking.

GRANDMA'S CUPCAKES IN MY BRAIN.

WHAT ABOUT CUPCAKES?

ME FILLED WITH JOY ABOUT THINKING OF A NEW IDEA.

Now everyone was talking again. But not everyone was excited. Miss Lois pointed at me and said, "Just Grace, you know better than to shout." I looked down. She was right. I looked over at Mimi for a smile to make me feel better, but she wasn't smiling. She was glaring at me. And then I knew. A horrible and terrible thing had just happened!

THE TERRIBLE THING

I'd done that exact thing that I'd promised Mimi I wouldn't do. Now my new idea was fighting Mimi's idea. And Mimi was probably thinking it was all on purpose. But it wasn't;

it was an accident. I looked up. Miss Lois was writing the word *cupcakes* right under the word *candy*.

WHAT I WAS HOPING FOR

That someone was going to give Miss Lois a suggestion that was even better than cupcakes or candy. If that happened and the class picked the new suggestion, then maybe Mimi wouldn't be mad at me. I looked around the room. There was only one hand up—it was Ruth's. Miss Lois pointed at her and I held my breath. I closed my eyes and tried to think good thoughts.

"Pickles," said Ruth. Suddenly I felt sick. Pickles was not a good suggestion. Pickles could not beat cupcakes. Miss Lois didn't think so either, because even though she wrote it down, she said, "Okay, no more food items please!" And then after that, there were no more hands up. I couldn't look at Mimi. I felt guilty. Why didn't I say superpowers like I was supposed to? I had no idea why my mouth had said what it did. But I knew what Mimi was thinking. She was thinking I was happy about it. She didn't know I was sorry and wishing that it had never happened.

BEING UNCOMFORTABLE

It's no fun to know that something bad is coming up and then to have to sit there and watch the bad thing happen right in front of you. Before we started the voting, Miss Lois told us the voting rules. "You only have one vote per person," she said. "If you like an idea put your hand up, and I will count the hands and write the number of votes next to it." And then, because a lot of kids don't pay attention, she said, "You can only put your hand up one time. You cannot vote more than once." She looked around the class to see if anyone looked confused, and then she said, "Okay, let's start."

Some ideas didn't get any votes. When Miss Lois said "Monkeys," no hands went up. But when Miss Lois said "Candy," a lot of hands went up. I put my hand up too, and crossed my fingers—maybe candy would win. Miss Lois counted the hands and wrote the number on the board.

Cupcakes was next. When Miss Lois asked for hands, I looked down at the floor.

I didn't want to know how many hands were up. I heard Miss Lois write the number on the board and then the class cheered. I didn't have to look up to know what had happened. Cupcakes had won.

I WON!

CAN A WINNER FEEL TERRIBLE?

YES! And sometimes a winner can even wish, with all her heart, that she was not the winner. If I were at home, I would have run up to my bedroom and made that exact wish while holding my last lucky penny.

THE LUCKY PENNY I WISHED I COULD BE HOLDING.

WHAT MISS LOIS DID NEXT

Miss Lois erased everything and then wrote the word *CUPCAKES* in big letters right in the middle of the board. It was hard to believe, but every second, things were getting worse. If I had asked the universe, "Is it going to get better?" the universe would have said, "I'm sorry, but the answer to that is NO!"

"Now let's put you all into groups," said Miss Lois. Everyone groaned. Nobody likes to be *put* into groups. "Can't we pick our own groups?" asked Owen 2. Miss Lois looked surprised. Owen 2 hardly ever asks questions. Miss Lois thought for a minute and then said yes, though it was a yes with a *but* attached to it.

BUT I LIKE TO MAKE THINGS COMPLICATED.

WHAT THE BUT WAS

Miss Lois said, "We're going to choose the group leaders randomly, but after that I'll let you pick the rest of your team." Miss Lois put everyone's name in a bowl and then pulled out six pieces of paper. "Owen 1, Grace F., Mimi, Owen 2, Marta, and Abigail. You are the group leaders," said Miss Lois. "Please come and stand at the front of the class." When they were all there Miss Lois said, "We'll do this in order. Each of you can pick one person until everyone is on a team. Owen 1, you can start."

Owen 1 picked Robert Walters, and Grace F. picked Grace L., but the big surprise was Mimi's turn. She picked Sunni. Nobody said anything, but I could tell that everyone was shocked. They were all thinking, *Why didn't she pick Grace?* I was the only one who knew the answer.

Sunni is not my favorite person, so I was pretty sure Mimi picked her on purpose to punish me! My face felt hot. I knew it was red. I looked down at my desk to hide it. I don't know if it was true or not, but I felt like everyone was staring at me. When it was Mimi's next turn, she picked Sammy. Grace F. looked at me from the front of the room and moved her eyebrows up and down. I could tell that she was asking if I wanted her to pick me. I nodded and then slumped in my seat. At least being on Grace F.'s team would be okay. But that didn't happen, because when it was Owen 1's turn, he picked me!

THE HORRIBLE SURPRISE

I couldn't believe it. Out of all the teams standing at the front, his was the one team I really, really, really did NOT want to be on, and now I was on it. Even being on Mimi's team with her being mad at me would have been better. I shook my head. Any team with Owen 1 and Robert Walters on it was not a good team—it was a disaster team!

Grace F. looked at me and shrugged. I stood up. It was not easy to make my feet walk over and stand next to Owen 1. Mimi picked Max next. Sammy and Max were best friends, and they'd been on a team with Mimi before, so that made sense.

The last person to be on our team was Ruth. She's a girl, but she's friends with Owen 1 and Robert Walters and pretty much acts just like them, so that wasn't any better for me. I had one new big feeling about the fair—*IT WAS GOING TO BE A NIGHTMARE!*

OUR CLASS PROJECT

After everyone was in a group, Miss Lois explained what we were going to do next. Each group had three things they had to do for the fair.

1. Make up a carnival game that had something to do with the theme of cupcakes.
2. Work at the fair at their game from eleven to twelve-thirty. After that, our part of the fair was going to be closed and we could go and do other stuff.
3. Compete as a team in the Cupcake Challenge.

WHAT IS THE CUPCAKE CHALLENGE?

Miss Lois's class always has a challenge. Anyone in third grade can enter a team and do it, but if you are in her class you don't have a choice: you have to do it. Last year it was the Bird Challenge, and the year before that it was the Pets Challenge. Miss Lois and the gym teacher, Mr. Clausen, make up the challenge, and it's always some kind of fun obstacle course or relay race. Last year the winners got to have their pictures in the front hall of the school for a whole week, plus they got special prize T-shirts.

Some people might think that winning the challenge is not a big deal, but they would be wrong. Winning the challenge is important, and probably one of the biggest things that can happen to you in third grade. Everyone in our class wants to win it!

WHAT OUR TEAM HAD ABSOLUTELY NO CHANCE OF

Winning the Cupcake Challenge.

WHAT OWEN 1 TOLD ME

After Miss Lois finished explaining everything, she said we could meet with our groups. Our group met at Owen 1's desk, which was the only good thing that had happened all afternoon. It was good because Owen 1 sits right behind me, so for our meeting I at least got to sit in my own chair. It wasn't a big good thing, but when only bad things are happening to you, you notice the good things even if they are super tiny.

As soon as we were all sitting down, Owen 1 looked at me and said, "I picked you because you are good at drawing and you like superheroes. So you can draw a really good Spider-Man for our game." "That's awesome," said Robert, and he high-fived Owen 1, then Ruth, and finally he tried to high-five me, but I ignored him. I was thinking about Owen 1's idea and getting more and more unhappy by the second. Spider-Man was a terrible idea and I couldn't wait to tell him why.

WHAT I TOLD HIM

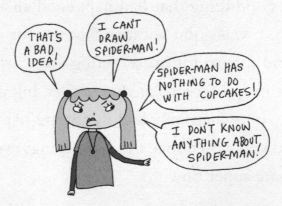

Owen 1 wasn't listening to me, because the next thing he said was "It'll be great. I'll show you pictures. You can copy them." I turned around and looked at the front of the room. I felt like crying. Here was the best thing of the whole year finally happening, and it was ruined. It was supposed to be fun and exciting and amazing, and instead it was going to be none of those things. It was going to be horrible.

HOW MISS LOIS SAVED ME

Miss Lois was walking around the room listening to all the groups talk about what they wanted to do. After about two minutes at our group she said, "Remember, class, your game has to have something to do with cupcakes." Owen 1 banged his hand on the desk. "That ruins everything!" he complained. I smiled. It was the only smile I'd had all afternoon.

I looked across at Mimi. She caught me looking. I turned away. Two seconds later I heard her laugh really loud. I know Mimi, so I could tell that it was a fake laugh. It was a laugh to make me unhappy and it worked 100 percent.

WHAT I WAS KNOWING

That I was going to be walking home alone.

As soon as the bell rang I packed up my stuff super fast and raced out of the room. I did not want to be walking home behind

Max, Sammy, and Mimi. I ran all the way to the edge of the schoolyard before I stopped and walked. I was the only one on the sidewalk. Being alone by yourself is better than being alone when there are lots of people around you, especially if all the other people are together in a group.

When I got home Mr. Scruffers jumped all over me like usual. It was exactly what I needed. Mr. Scruffers could be one of those dogs that visit sick people, because just being with her can make you feel better.

DOCTOR GIVING HIS PRESCRIPTION

I LOOKED AT YOUR CHART AND I RECOMMEND TWENTY MINUTES OF MR. SCRUFFERS'S LOVE AS THERAPY.

MY NEW IDEA

After playing with Mr. Scruffers, I decided to make Mimi an apology letter, and not just a normal apology letter, but an amazing apology letter. Making this kind of letter takes a long time. If someone ever gave me one, I would know right away how sorry she was, because if someone spends a long time to make a letter, then she is very, very sorry and you should probably forgive her.

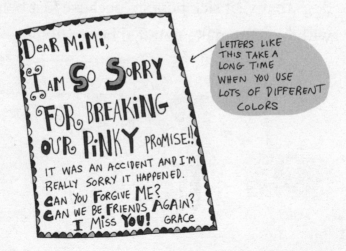

Dear Mimi,
I am So Sorry FOR BREAKING OUR PINKY PROMISE!!
IT WAS AN ACCIDENT AND I'M REALLY SORRY IT HAPPENED. CAN YOU FORGIVE ME? CAN WE BE FRIENDS AGAIN? I MiSS YOU! GRACE

LETTERS LIKE THIS TAKE A LONG TIME WHEN YOU USE LOTS OF DIFFERENT COLORS

After I finished the letter I found a box and put my two favorite cupcakes and the letter inside it, and took it over to Mimi's house. I was too nervous to see her, so I put it on the step, rang the doorbell, and then ran home super fast. After she read the letter, I just knew she would forgive me. She'd either come over or call me, so I waited downstairs so I could be close to the door and the phone. Since I had nothing to do but wait, I got my drawing stuff out and drew a comic. Drawing comics usually makes me feel better if I am sad, but this time it didn't work that way. It just made me feel more anxious for Mimi to call.

After about an hour I told Mom to yell for me
if the phone rang, and I went upstairs to my

room. After about two hours, I got worried that no one at Mimi's house had heard me ring the doorbell. Maybe the cupcakes and the letter were still sitting outside on the step. I took Mr. Scrufffers on a walk around the block so I could check, but when we walked by Mimi's house and looked, there was nothing at her door. The box was gone.

THE DOORBELL I USED

MIMI'S FRONT DOOR

NO BOX

After about three hours, I had some new thoughts. These new thoughts were not good, so I told myself not to think about them, and I went into the living room and watched TV with Mom and Dad. After four hours, the thoughts came back. Sometimes it takes a long time for your brain to believe something, especially if it is something you don't want to believe. I didn't want to believe what my brain was telling me, but after four hours I kind of had to.

MIMI IS NOT GOING TO FORGIVE ME.

FEELINGS

At first I was really sad. Mr. Scruffers is a good pillow when your eyes are full of tears. She knew something was wrong, and even though she couldn't fix it, just having her be there with me made it feel a little better. That's probably why Mom wanted me in the car with her after taking Grandma to the airport. It's nice to have someone with you when you are sad. After a while I stopped crying. I was glad about that, because I was getting tired of blowing my nose every five seconds.

Mr. Scruffers was looking at me like she wanted to know what was wrong, so I started to tell her about everything that had happened. She likes it when I talk to her, and she's a good listener as long as you don't say one of her jump-up-and-get-excited words. As I was telling the story, something strange happened—my sad started turning into mad—and not just a little mad, but really mad.

MY REASONS FOR BEING MAD

1. I made a special note for Mimi and she didn't even say anything about it.

2. I said "cupcakes" by accident. It just popped into my head. If people say something by accident, you should forgive them. Because an accident is not the same as on purpose.

3. She took the cupcakes I gave her and probably ate them. If you are not going to forgive someone, you shouldn't eat their cupcakes. You should give them back.

But mostly I was mad because of this.

RAYS OF ANGER

IF MIMI CAN'T FORGIVE ME THAT MEANS SHE WASN'T A VERY GOOD FRIEND IN THE FIRST PLACE.

WHAT IS NOT GOOD

It's not a nice feeling to go to sleep angry, but sometimes you just can't help it. Before I went to bed I picked up the superhero guessing ball and threw it in my closet. I didn't care if it was super cool—it was from Mimi and I didn't want to look at it.

THE NEXT MORNING

I asked Mom to make me French toast for breakfast. Today was a day I was definitely going to need extra energy. Working on a carnival game with Owen 1, Robert Walters, and Ruth was not going to be easy. But Mom said, "I don't have time to make French toast, but here, I got you these French toast granola bars. I bet they're just as good."

WHAT WAS NOT DELICIOUS

The French toast granola bar. Any time something is pretending to taste like something it's not, you probably shouldn't eat it.

I left for school five minutes early. I didn't want to walk out the door and see Mimi walking ahead of me. On the walk to school I got madder and madder with every step.

WHAT IS HARD TO DO

Keep it a secret that you and your best friend are not talking to each other. Of course everyone knew. Some people asked me about it, but I wouldn't tell anyone anything.

WHAT WAS A SURPRISE

Owen 1 was still upset about yesterday and not getting to do his Spider-Man idea. "Spider-Man's my favorite," he said. "I don't want to do anything else." He put his head on his desk and stayed quiet. I didn't want to feel sorry for him, but my empathy feelings started working and I couldn't help it. I have a mini superpower: whenever someone is sad or unhappy my brain makes me do whatever I can to help that person. Usually that's not a bad thing, but Owen 1 was someone who was not my favorite, so that made it more complicated.

MY OUTSIDE FEELINGS DON'T LIKE OWEN 1, BUT MY INSIDE FEELINGS WANT TO HELP HIM

"Maybe we can still make it a Spider-Man game," I said. Owen 1 didn't look up. "Can it be a strength thing?" asked Robert. "Sure," I said. I took out a piece of paper and wrote down the word *strength*. It wasn't much, but it was a start. "How can we do that with cupcakes?" asked Ruth. I had no idea. "Let's figure out the game first, and then we can do the cupcake part later," I said. "Can it be a throwing game?" asked Owen 1. Suddenly he was interested. I wrote down the word *throwing* next to *strength*. "What's next?" asked Ruth. I looked up. They were all looking at me. I don't know how it happened, but I could tell that something had changed—suddenly I had become the team leader.

THE CARNIVAL GAME

Inventing a carnival game was not easy—especially with my group. I spent a lot of time saying, "No, we can't do that."

THINGS I HAD TO SAY NO TO
Throwing really heavy weights
Throwing real darts
Throwing anything big
Throwing sticks
Throwing rocks
Throwing anything pointy

Finally Owen 1 got mad and threw his hands in the air. "What can we throw? Balloons!" He banged his fists on his desk. I looked over at Miss Lois. She was watching us, but she didn't get up. We were safe for now. I didn't want Owen 1 to get sent to the not-paying-attention chair. We needed him to help with the game. Suddenly I had a thought. Maybe balloons were a good idea. I wrote down the word *balloons*. Owen 1 looked up. "Can they be water balloons?" he asked. Ruth looked at Owen 1 and shook her head. "Even I know the answer to that," she said. I looked at her and smiled. It was nice not to be the one saying no.

NO, OF COURSE YOU CAN'T HAVE WATER BALLOONS!

WHAT WAS A SURPRISE

Miss Lois telling us it was time to stop working for the day. I couldn't believe it was already time to go home. "We won't work on these again until Thursday," she said. The whole class groaned. Working on carnival games was a lot more fun than regular work. I looked over at Mimi but she was talking to Sammy. Before we left, Miss Lois gave us all forms to take home. The top half was for explaining our assignment, and the bottom half was a tear-off sheet for our parents about signing up as volunteers. Every family was supposed to have a least one parent be a helper for the fair. I knew who was going to do it in my family—Mom loves to volunteer.

I LIKE TO DO MY PART TO HELP THE SCHOOL.

THE SURPRISE INSIDE

Mr. Scruffers was not at the door when I got home. This was unusual. At first I was worried, but then Mom yelled, "She's in the backyard!" What she said next was the surprise part. "Robert is outside playing with her until his mother gets back. Where's Mimi? I thought she'd be with you." "I don't know," I said. I didn't want to tell Mom about us fighting. I tried to change the subject. "Here, you have to sign up for this." I pulled out the school fair flyer and waved it in the air. Mom took it without looking and put it on the counter. "I'll do it later," she said. "Go over and put a note on Mimi's door so she knows to come here when she gets home."

Having Mimi over was the last thing I wanted, but I couldn't say that. I pulled a piece of paper and a pencil out of my backpack and walked toward the door. "You can have a cupcake when she gets here," said

Mom. "Okay," I said. But I didn't want to think about Mimi or eating cupcakes.

CUPCAKES THAT ARE STILL
LEFT FROM MAKING THEM
WITH GRANDMA

THE SURPRISE OUTSIDE

When I opened the door Mimi was standing right outside. It was not what either of us was expecting. Mimi looked at the ground. "No one's home at my house," she said. "I know," I said. "You're supposed to come over here until your mom gets back. Robert's in the backyard." Mimi sighed. I pushed the door open wider, and she came in. "I'll get Robert," I said. Mimi didn't say anything.

As soon as I opened the back door Mr. Scruffers came running over to see me. She jumped up once, but then stopped. She was tired. Robert was good at using up her energy. "Hi, Grace!" shouted Robert. I waved back and said, "Do you want a cupcake?" He ran over. "You have the best cupcakes!" he said. "How do you know?" I asked. He didn't answer and raced past me to the kitchen. Mimi had probably given him one of my cupcakes. It was going to be hard not to say anything about that. I took a deep breath and followed him.

Mimi was already sitting at the table. Robert sat down next to her. I grabbed the plate of cupcakes and put it in the middle of the table. "I'm not hungry," said Mimi, and she crossed her arms. "Well, I am," said Robert. "I am too!" I said. I took a cupcake. "I want the kind with the gummy bears on top!" complained Robert. Mimi looked at Robert. "There aren't any with gummy bears," said Mimi. "Pick from what's here. Grace doesn't have any gummy bears." "Yes, she does!" said Robert. He was getting mad. "They were on the other cupcakes!" Suddenly Robert covered up his mouth with his hands.

WHAT IS EASY TO TELL

It's not easy to tell if a grownup is lying, but little kids are different. They aren't good at it yet, so it's easier. Mimi and I both looked at Robert and we both had the same question. "What other cupcakes?" Robert looked up at us, and then all of a sudden he started to cry. "It was an accident," he sobbed. Mimi was confused. She had no idea what Robert was talking about, but I did. My brain was slowly figuring it out.

ROBERT, DID YOU FIND TWO CUPCAKES IN A BOX?

Robert nodded his head. "Here," I said. I gave him the cupcake in my hand. It didn't have gummy bears on it, but it worked. He stopped crying and took a bite. "What's going on?" asked Mimi. She looked at Robert again, but he didn't say anything—his mouth was full of cupcake. She shook her head and looked at me. I took a deep breath, and then told her about the box with the apology letter and the cupcakes. "You wrote me a letter?" she asked. I nodded. "You ate my cupcakes?" she asked. Robert nodded.

Mimi looked back and forth at both of us, like she couldn't believe what she was hearing, and then suddenly, she looked at Robert. "Where's the letter?" she asked. Robert looked down and shook his head. "Did you throw it in the garbage?" she asked. I held my breath and crossed my fingers. *Please say no.*

IT WAS AN ACCIDENT.

I needed Mimi to see that letter. Robert shook his head. I breathed again, but Mimi wasn't finished. "Is it gone?" she asked.

He nodded. How? I wondered. Two seconds later I knew the answer. "Did you flush it down the toilet?" asked Mimi. Robert didn't move. He looked scared.

WHAT HAPPENED NEXT

I didn't want to wait for what was going to happen next. I didn't want to take any chances. I ran upstairs, grabbed Grandma's pot, and took out the last penny. I held it tight in my hand and made a wish.

PLEASE, PLEASE LET MIMI FORGIVE ME!

WISHING ENERGY

WHAT WAS LUCKY

The penny. When I opened my eyes Mimi was standing in the doorway, looking at me. "I'm sorry," she said. "I thought you didn't want to be friends anymore." "Of course I did," I said. "I made you a special apology letter." And then because I wanted Mimi to know how really sorry I was, I told her all about it.

WHAT WAS ALSO LUCKY

When Mimi and I came back downstairs, we were friends again. Robert was still in the kitchen, and still eating cupcakes! "How many have you eaten?" asked Mimi. I looked at the plate. Almost all of them were gone. "No more!" said Mimi, and she snatched the one he was holding out of his hand. I think he was too surprised to complain. "You're lucky you're not sick!" she said. "And you're also lucky that Grace is going to forgive you for flushing her letter down the toilet." Robert looked at the ground. I didn't know what to say, so I just nodded.

MY LETTER

"I think I'll eat this one," said Mimi. She looked at the cupcake she was holding. She'd gotten it away from Robert before he'd even had a chance to bite it. "I'll have one too," I said, and I took the last one from the plate. For a second I thought about saying, *High-five for cupcakes!*, but then I changed my mind. That really wasn't the right thing to say, especially after everything that had happened. I took a bite and said something else. It was perfect.

YUMMY + DELICIOUS =

CATCHING UP

Mimi and I had a lot of catching up to do. We had two days of not talking to make up for. I told her all about Owen 1 and how I was feeling a little bit better about being in his group. She said she was surprised to hear that and I said I was surprised to say that, and then we both laughed. After that Mimi told me all about her group. They already had a plan for their

entire carnival game. They were not like us—
we were still trying to figure out what to do.

THAT NIGHT

Mimi and I flashed our bedroom lights on and
off at each other. It had been a long time since
we'd done it. We usually flash three or four
times. When it was my turn, I said a word for
each flash. Even though Mimi couldn't hear
me it felt like the right thing to do.

WHAT MAKES A DAY EXTRA HARD

Knowing that you won't get to work on the
fair for even one minute of school time. Even

Owen 2 complained. I thought that might make a difference, but Miss Lois just said, "Let's concentrate on our work. We'll have lots of time to think about the fair tomorrow."

Everyone noticed that Mimi and I were friends again, and even though a lot of people asked, we didn't tell them one thing about why it had happened. Some things the world does not need to know.

MORE FAIR WORK

On Thursday I woke up late and had to hurry to meet Mimi. When I got downstairs Mom handed me one of those terrible French toast granola bars to eat on the way. It was better than nothing, but not much better.

Mimi and I had to rush to make it on time. It's kind of hard to talk while you're running, but Mimi was able to tell me one important thing. She was going to Philadelphia with her family for the weekend. I was sad about that, but I didn't complain. Losing Mimi for only two days was a lot better than losing her forever!

After the announcements were over, Miss Lois let us work in our groups. "Look what we brought," said Ruth. Both she and Owen 1 held up balloons. "If we blow them up, we can maybe get some more ideas about our game," said Owen 1. "Okay," I said. If Miss Lois didn't like it, then she could tell us to stop. I was tired of saying no.

EXPERIMENTS WITH THE BALLOONS

1. Balloons are not easy to throw—they just kind of float.

"Maybe we should tie something on the end of it," said Robert. "Then it will be heavier and easier to throw." There weren't a lot of choices. We tried a pencil, but that was too light. "We could use my pencil case," said Ruth. "It has two pencils and this eraser in it." I was just tying the pencil case to the bottom of the balloon when Miss Lois came over. "You're working so well together," she said.

"But maybe you could save the experimenting part of your project to do at home. You could meet after school or on the weekend." Everyone in my group was surprised except me. I had a feeling we weren't going to be allowed to be throwing balloons around in the classroom. None of the other groups were doing stuff like that.

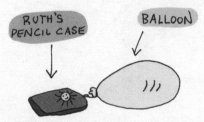

"What a rip-off!" said Owen 1. "Where are we going to practice?" complained Ruth. Without even thinking I said, "You can come to my house." "When?" asked Robert. "Today?" Today was too soon. I needed to ask Mom about it first. "Uh . . . how about Saturday," I said. "Okay," said Owen 1, "I guess that's better than nothing." I frowned. Better than nothing? No wonder Owen 1 always got in trouble. He had terrible manners.

MY HOUSE IS A LOT BETTER THAN NOTHING.

LUNCHTIME

At lunch Mimi told me that she was having her group over to her house too. "They're coming on Friday," she said. "And you can come too. We're going to have pizza." I had three thoughts.

MY THOUGHTS

1. They don't need me there.
2. Mimi's group is better than my group.
3. I really like pizza.

Sometimes if you are feeling a little sorry for yourself you can say the wrong thing. This was almost one of those times, but I stopped myself before it happened. "Okay," I said. "I'll come for pizza." "Oh, good," said Mimi. "Now it'll be more fun." "I wish you could come to my group on Saturday," I said. Mimi smiled and shook her head.

There was a big difference between hanging out with her group and hanging out with my group. She was probably thinking she was lucky that she was going to be away in Philadelphia.

WHAT HAPPENED IN THE AFTERNOON

Miss Lois made us do regular schoolwork. There was a lot of groaning and complaining. But before she made us do math, she showed us the cupcake crowns she had made for the winners of the Cupcake Challenge.

CUPCAKE CROWN

THAT NIGHT

Nothing exciting happened, except that I told Mom about having Owen 1, Robert Walters, and Ruth over on Saturday. Mom said she was sure everything would turn out fine. That was easy for her to say—she'd never met them.

Now with Mimi being gone there wasn't anything fun to look forward to for the whole weekend.

FRIDAYS ARE THE BEST DAYS EVEN IF NOTHING AMAZING HAPPENS, BECAUSE IN YOUR BRAIN YOU KNOW THAT TOMORROW YOU DON'T HAVE TO GO TO SCHOOL

THE GOOD THINGS THAT HAPPENED TODAY

1. I had lunch with Mimi and Sunni. This was a double surprise because I'd never

eaten lunch with Sunni before, and the second part of the surprise was that she was actually pretty nice.

2. Miss Lois let us work with our groups for the last half of the afternoon. Since we still didn't know what we were going to do for our game, we just mostly sat around and watched everyone else. I was really hoping that working with the balloons on Saturday was going to help us figure out what to do. Otherwise we were going to be in big trouble.

THOSE BALLOONS HAVE TO SAVE US.

After school I walked home with Mimi, Sammy, Max, and Sunni. It was a little weird having Sunni there, but by the time we got to my house I was used to it. "What time is pizza?" I asked. "Five-thirty," said Mimi, "but you can come over at five." "Okay," I said. "I'll see you later." I watched them all go into Mimi's house, and then I went inside. I knew it was wrong, but I couldn't help it. I was feeling a little sad and a little jealous.

SAD + JEALOUS = SADLOUS

Being with Mr. Scruffers helped. Most of the sad went away, but the jealous part was harder to get rid of. I guess jealousy is stickier.

MIMI'S HOUSE

At five o'clock I went over to Mimi's house. When I saw their game I couldn't believe how good it was. It was excellent. "It's called Candy Toss," said Sunni. "Who made all the candy?" I asked. "Mimi and Sunni," said Sammy. "Max and I painted the cupcakes." "Did you know Sunni can sew?" asked Mimi. "Once I showed her how, she did a really good job." Sunni looked down and her face turned red. It was the first time I had ever seen her embarrassed.

A ladder was set up next to the board with the cupcakes painted on it. Sammy was standing on top of it. "Hey, Max—throw me the candy," he said. Max tossed it to him. "I'm going to try the game from up here," said Sammy. He leaned over and dropped the candy onto the cupcakes. Each piece landed perfectly, right in the middle of the frosting part on the cupcake.

THE CANDY TOSS GAME

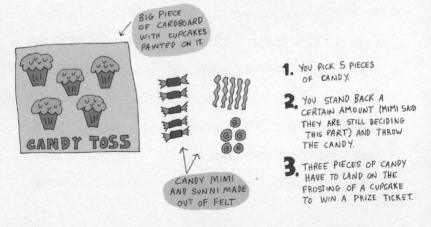

BIG PIECE OF CARDBOARD WITH CUPCAKES PAINTED ON IT.

CANDY TOSS

CANDY MIMI AND SUNNI MADE OUT OF FELT

1. YOU PICK 5 PIECES OF CANDY.

2. YOU STAND BACK A CERTAIN AMOUNT (MIMI SAID THEY ARE STILL DECIDING THIS PART) AND THROW THE CANDY.

3. THREE PIECES OF CANDY HAVE TO LAND ON THE FROSTING OF A CUPCAKE TO WIN A PRIZE TICKET.

"It's good we're not using the ladder for the game," said Sammy. "It's too easy." I picked up a piece of candy and threw it. I missed the board completely. "It's not easy from the ground," I said. Both Sammy and Max smiled. It was a good game.

After our pizza dinner everyone had to go home. Mimi had to go to bed early because she was leaving at six in the morning for her trip. That night Mimi and I flashed our lights at each other eight times—four for tonight, and four for tomorrow night when she was going to be gone.

SATURDAY

I didn't really have much to do to get ready for the group to come over, but still I was nervous about it. Mom said she would get some balloons from the store, and I got the art supplies and cardboard and paper out. I tried to think of a great idea for our game, but all I could think about was Mimi's game and how good it was.

As two o'clock got closer I started to feel more and more nervous. It was strange to have people I didn't know very well coming over. I would have felt a lot better if Mimi was with me too. The first person to arrive was Robert Walters. I am lucky that he is a huge dog fan, or we would have had nothing to talk about. As soon as he heard Mr. Scruffers barking in the backyard, he wanted to go outside and see her. Then once he met her, he wanted to throw the ball for her. I thought he might say something about it being weird that she was a girl dog with a boy name, but he didn't. "I wish I could have a dog," he said. He didn't even mind touching her slob-bery ball.

← ROBERT WALTERS'S HAND

← MR. SCRUFFERS'S BALL

Ruth and Owen 1 came about ten minutes later. Robert wanted to start playing with the balloons, but I said that Mom was getting them and she wasn't back from the store yet. Dad came outside to check on us, so I introduced him to everyone. He already knew all about Owen 1 because I complain about him a lot, but he didn't say anything. Grownups are good about not saying stuff that could hurt other people's feelings.

"Does your dog do any tricks?" asked Owen 1. "Just one," I said. "But it's not very exciting. All she does is sit." "Can we see?" asked Ruth. "Okay," I said. I took the ball from Robert, held it high in the air, and said, "Sit, Mr. Scruffers. Sit." For a second she just stood there and didn't do anything, but then she sat down. "Can she shake?" asked Robert. Without waiting for an answer, he bent down and grabbed her paw. Instantly Mr. Scruffers fell over. "That's so cool," said Owen 1. "It's like you zapped her. Like you have a superpower. How did you do that?" "I didn't do anything," said Robert. She just did it by herself. "Wow!" said Owen 1. "That's the coolest dog!"

Robert and Owen 1 each tried the trick with Mr. Scruffers about three or four times. They loved it. Mr. Scruffers could do a cool trick and I didn't even know it.

MOM'S MISTAKE

Mom came out of the garage a few seconds later. Right away I could see that she had bought the wrong kind of balloons. I forgot to tell her to get the kind you blow up yourself. "I had to go to three stores to get these," she said. After all that trouble there was no way I could tell her they were wrong, so all I said was thank you.

I tied the balloons to a chair so they wouldn't fly away, and then we talked about what to do next. "I brought my pencil case," said Ruth. "Let's see if it works," I said. I took one of the balloons and tied Ruth's pencil case to it. "It needs to be heavier," I said. Ruth found some stones and we put them inside the case.

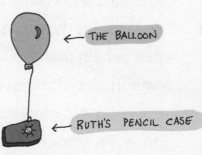

"Now let me try throwing it," said Owen 1. He grabbed the balloon and tried to throw it, but his arm got tangled in the string. "Stupid balloon," said Owen 1. He tried to kick it but missed. It was hard not to laugh. "I'll hit it for you," said Robert. He threw Mr. Scruffers's ball at the balloon. It whacked against the balloon and pushed the balloon and the pencil case a few feet away. "Let me try that," said Owen 1. It worked for him too.

"Let's have a race," yelled Robert. He grabbed another balloon and tied some sticks to the bottom of it. Then he put both balloons next to each other, and grabbed one of Mr. Scruffers's other balls. "I'll hit the red one and you hit the green one," said Robert. "The first person that gets their balloon to that bush over there is the winner," said Owen 1. I shook my head. No wonder they never got anything done at school. They didn't know how to

STOP!

concentrate. We were supposed to be working on our carnival game, not racing balloons.

Everyone was surprised to hear me yelling. But they were even more surprised when I told them why. "That's it!" I said. "You just invented the carnival game!" "We did?" they asked. I nodded and pointed to the balloons. "Now all we have to do is make it a Spider-Man cupcake theme."

It took a while for everyone to agree on what to do, but by five o'clock we had our game all finished. I was surprised. It actually turned out pretty good. This time when Robert Walters said he wanted to high-five, I let him hit my hand. The only thing I was not super excited about was the name, but everyone else liked it so I said, "Okay." Sometimes you just have to go with the group, even if you think they are making a not excellent choice.

SPIDER-MAN VERSUS THE
CUPCAKE MONSTER

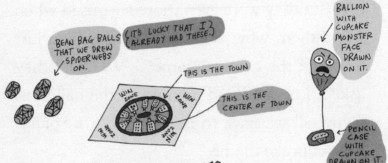

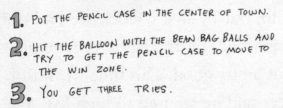

HOW TO PLAY

1. PUT THE PENCIL CASE IN THE CENTER OF TOWN.

2. HIT THE BALLOON WITH THE BEAN BAG BALLS AND TRY TO GET THE PENCIL CASE TO MOVE TO THE WIN ZONE.

3. YOU GET THREE TRIES.

I didn't know it while it was happening, but working with my group was the most fun I was going to have all weekend.

WHAT HAPPENED THE REST OF THE WEEKEND

Nothing—it was boring. I missed Mimi, but I did come up with three superpowers that the superpower ball couldn't guess.

1. Empathy Power
2. Balloon Power—you can float like a balloon.
3. Slobber Power—you slobber on things to keep people from touching them.

FOUR EXCITING THINGS THAT HAPPENED ON MONDAY

1. Mimi told me about her trip to Philadelphia. She said she had a great time. Her three favorite things were visiting the aquarium, seeing the Liberty Bell, and visiting an old prison. She said the

prison was really interesting, but the best thing was touching a shark at the aquarium. It was only a baby shark, but still that was pretty cool.

2. Miss Lois wore her finished cupcake hat so we could all see it.

3. Sandra Orr's mom brought in a giant cupcake costume for someone to wear on the day of the fair. She said it was an old Halloween costume, but it was perfect for our carnival.

REALLY GREAT HAT.

4. Miss Lois said she needed families to volunteer to make cupcakes. Right away my hand went up. I had to—I had the best cupcake recipe in the entire world.

This was a lot of exciting news to have in one day.

Before we left, Miss Lois reminded us that we needed to turn in our project plans and our parent volunteer forms. She said, "I'm assigning parent volunteer jobs this week. I need those forms."

WHAT MIMI AND I TALKED ABOUT ON THE WAY HOME

As soon as I got home I reminded Mom about the form she had to fill out and then I put my group's project plan in my backpack by the front door. I didn't want to forget it for tomorrow. We'd done a much better job than I thought we would. It was surprising, but I even felt proud of it. I smiled, gave it one last look, and then ran outside to the backyard to see Mr. Scruffers.

WHAT WAS A SURPRISE ON TUESDAY

Miss Lois picked our project plan as the model to show the class. It was a good thing that we'd included a description about how to play our game. A lot of other teams had forgotten about that part.

On the way home I invited Mimi over to see Mr. Scruffers's new trick, but she said she had to fix some of the candy beanbags for her carnival game. "Sunni's not really that great a sewer," she said. "Oh," I said. Maybe that's why she had been blushing. At school Sunni is good at everything, so it was kind of nice to find out she isn't perfect.

IT'S EASIER TO LIKE SOMEONE WHEN THEY ARE NOT PERFECT AT EVERYTHING.

THE TWO FUN THINGS THAT HAPPENED ON WEDNESDAY AFTER SCHOOL

1. I showed Mimi Mr. Scruffers's new trick. She loved it. She could hardly believe that Robert had figured it out. He had found a new trick where we thought

there was nothing. That was pretty amazing.

2. Mimi and I made a list of all the ingredients we needed to make forty-eight cupcakes. It was lucky that Mom had bought a ton of cupcake stuff when Grandma was visiting—she hardly needed to buy anything new at all.

OUR LIST FOR WHAT MOM NEEDED TO BUY.

-CUPCAKE LINERS
-EGGS

THURSDAY

Miss Lois said that even though the fair was starting at eleven in the morning on Saturday, we had to come to school at nine-thirty with our carnival games. "You are going to need time to set them up and get everything ready," she said. I couldn't wait. Fair Day was almost here!

WHAT WAS FUN

We spent the afternoon making signs for our games. It was kind of like being excited for a birthday party, but different. For birthday parties you don't get I-hope-I-don't-mess-up feelings.

THE SIGN FOR OUR GAME

SPIDER-MAN VERSUS THE CUPCAKE MONSTER

FRIDAY

My first thought this morning was *only one more day until the fair.* Today was going to feel like a long day. I just knew it. That's what always happens when you are excited about something that isn't going to happen until the next day.

While I was eating breakfast the phone rang. "It's probably Mimi," I said. "I bet she's excited too." I picked up the phone, but it wasn't Mimi—it was for Mom.

"Who is it?" whispered Mom. I shrugged my shoulders.

MOM TALKING ON THE PHONE →

OF COURSE I'D LIKE TO HELP.

YES, YES, A SPECIAL JOB? WONDERFUL, I UNDERSTAND.

OKAY. I'LL BE THERE ON SATURDAY. THANK YOU FOR CALLING.

It wasn't hard to guess what Mom was talking about. When she got off the phone she said, "How embarrassing. I should have gotten that form in." "What was it?" I asked. "It was about volunteering for the fair," said Mom. "They need me for a special job." "Maybe you're going to be one of the money moms," I said. "Us kids aren't suppose to do stuff with the tickets or money." Mom smiled. "Whatever it is, I'm sure it'll be fun."

Then she said, "What would you like for breakfast?" "Anything but those French toast bars," I said. "They're horrible!"

WHAT HAPPENED AT SCHOOL

Miss Lois is smart. She could tell right away

that our class was not going to be any good at doing regular schoolwork. So instead of working, we made decorations for the fair. My favorite thing was the stuffed cupcakes. I made three of them and would have made more, but Miss Lois ran out of staples for the stapler.

HOW TO MAKE A STUFFED CUPCAKE

1. CUT OUT A CUPCAKE SHAPE. YOU NEED TWO OF THEM.

2. DECORATE BOTH SIDES LIKE A CUPCAKE.

3. STAPLE AROUND EDGE BUT LEAVE A SPACE OPEN.
← STAPLES
LEAVE THIS PART OPEN

4. CRUMPLE UP PAPER AND STUFF THE CUPCAKE.
← NOW THE CUPCAKE LOOKS PUFFY

5. STAPLE THE BOTTOM AND HANG IT UP.

For the last part of the afternoon, Miss Lois let us all watch a movie about whales. It had nothing to do with cupcakes, but that was okay. It was still good.

THE CUPCAKE CHALLENGE

Right before we left, Miss Lois reminded everyone not to forget that we had to be back at school with our games at nine-thirty, and that the Cupcake Challenge was starting at three o'clock on the field behind the cafeteria. It was like saying, "Hey, your birthday's tomorrow—don't forget to come to the party." Everyone knew when it was, and where it was, and we all couldn't wait to be there.

WHAT HAPPENED ON THE WAY HOME

When Mimi and I were almost home I saw something shiny on the sidewalk. I looked down, and there right beside my foot was a lucky penny. It was the first one I'd found for Grandma's lucky penny pot.

As soon as I got home I ran upstairs and put the penny in the pot. It was nice to know that there was luck in there if I needed it.

MAKING CUPCAKES

Mimi came over after she dropped off her stuff at home. Mom said we could have pizza for dinner while we made the cupcakes. Both Mimi and I like the decorating part of cupcakes more than the making part of the cupcakes, so after the first ones were in the oven, Mom helped us by making the rest. We were pretty much too busy decorating to do the making part anyway.

WHAT IS AMAZING

The smell of cupcakes cooking in the oven. I could hardly wait for them to come out. Dad said we had to make more than forty-eight cupcakes because it wasn't fair to make the house smell delicious and then not leave any for him to eat. Mom just shook her head and said, "I guess we'll be making these all night." I didn't mind so much. It was nice to have something to do. It made time go by faster, because both Mimi and I couldn't wait for to-morrow to start.

WHAT TOOK A REALLY LONG TIME

Making and decorating all the cupcakes! The ones we made at the beginning were definite-ly fancier than the ones we made at the end. At least they were all going to be delicious—that part was good.

WHAT HAPPENED AT BEDTIME

Mimi and I flashed our lights at each other three times—one flash for each word in *Yay for tomorrow!*

ME FLASHING MY LIGHTS FOR MIMI

YAY FOR TOMORROW!

WHAT WAS HARD TO DO

Fall asleep. Even with Mr. Scruffers snuggled up close to me, I couldn't make myself feel sleepy. It's not easy to fall asleep when your brain is excited.

GETTING READY FOR THE SPRING FAIR

When I got up, Mom was already downstairs making French toast! "Real French toast for the Cupcake Challenge," said Mom, "so you have extra energy." I gave her a hug. It's good to let your parents know you're happy with them when they do something nice for you.

Mom's French toast was excellent, and 100 percent better than the horrible French toast granola bars she'd been giving me. After breakfast I got everything ready for the fair.

When we got to school, Mom helped me carry everything in to the activity room. The floor was covered with squares outlined with tape, and each square had the name of a team on it. It was easy to find my team's square, because my team was already standing in it.

"I'll see you later," said Mom. "I'll be back in an hour to do my volunteer shift." "Okay," I said.

The room was getting busier and busier every second. It was hard not to stop and stare at what everyone else was bringing in, but I forced myself to concentrate. We needed to get our game set up.

THE GAMES

After we put our game together, I went for a walk around the room to see what the other teams had done. There were some really good games.

WHAT HAPPENED AT TEN FORTY-FIVE

Miss Lois had us stand next to our games, and then she introduced each team to the parent volunteer that was going to help us. "The parent volunteer is the only person who can handle the tickets," said Miss Lois. "But other than that, I want you to run your own games." I thought Mom would be our parent volunteer, but I didn't see her anywhere. We got Owen 2's mom instead. Owen 2's mom is not like Owen 2—she likes to talk. After we introduced ourselves she said, "You can call me Colleen." I think we felt a little weird calling her Colleen, so we just called her "Owen 2's mom." She didn't seem to mind. "Can you show me how to play the game?" she asked. Owen 1 did the demonstrating. I could tell he was really excited, because he explained it a lot more than he needed to.

YOU USE THESE BOMB THINGS AND THROW THEM AT THE CUPCAKE MONSTER BALLOON. THE BALLOON IS THE BAD GUY AND...

WHAT HAPPENED AT ELEVEN

I couldn't believe it when Miss Lois said, "Get ready, kids—here come the customers." All of a sudden I felt a little bit worried, mixed in with my excited feelings.

EXCITED + WORRIED = EXORRIED

What if no one played our game? What if all the other games were busy except ours? I only had to worry for about two minutes, because as soon as little boys saw the name of our game, they wanted to play it. Owen 1 was right. Spider-Man vs. The Cupcake Monster was a good name. Little kids love Spider-Man.

WHAT I WAS LOOKING FOR

Even though we were really busy, I kept looking for Mom. I wanted her to see how popular our game was. I even snuck out into the hallway to see if I could find her. There were a lot of people out there, but Mom wasn't one of them. Someone was dressed up in the giant cupcake suit. The cupcake looked silly and cute at the same time. He was really friendly and when he saw me he gave me a super-big wave. I waved back and watched him for a second. People love giant dressed-up characters. I bet having him in the hallway was making people want to come in to see our games. He waved again and I smiled and went back to our game.

GIANT CUPCAKE
WAVING AT ME

When it got close to twelve, I started to wonder if Mom had forgotten to come back to the fair. Normally she'd never forget something like that, but she had been forgetting a lot of stuff lately.

WHERE IS MOM? I CAN'T BELIEVE SHE ISN'T HERE.

It was hard to concentrate on the game and be worried at the same time. Suddenly Owen 1 grabbed my arm, "Look!" he shouted. "It's the giant cupcake." "I know," I said. "I already saw it." I tried to ignore him. A little boy was playing our game, so I turned and watched him instead. "It's coming over here! Hi, giant cupcake!" shouted Owen 1.

He poked me in the arm. "Look!" I turned around to yell at him and there was the cupcake, only two steps away from me. It's hard not to be shocked when you suddenly have a giant cupcake staring right in your face.

Suddenly the cupcake grabbed me and gave me a big hug. "It's me!" said the cupcake. I tried to squirm away, but I couldn't—the cupcake had me in its grip. I could hear Owen 1 laughing behind me. "It's me, Mom!" said the cupcake. I stopped squirming. "Mom, are you in there?" I asked. "Yes," said the cupcake.

OH, MOM, I THOUGHT YOU DIDN'T COME.

"Look at my shoes." I looked down. The cupcake was wearing Mom's shoes. It was Mom! I gave the cupcake a giant hug back.

WHAT HAPPENED REALLY FAST

Suddenly Miss Lois announced that the Cupcake Games would be closing in five minutes. I couldn't believe it was already over. It was too bad that regular school didn't go by this fast.

After the last customer left, Miss Lois closed the door and said we could have fifteen minutes to go look at each other's games. "I'm not going anywhere," said Owen 1. "Our game is the best, so I'm going to stay right here and guard it." I shook my head. No one was going to steal our game, but it was nice that he loved it so much. If he wanted to, he could take it home. Even though we'd used stuff from my house to make it, I didn't need to keep it.

MY FAVORITE GAMES THAT I SAW

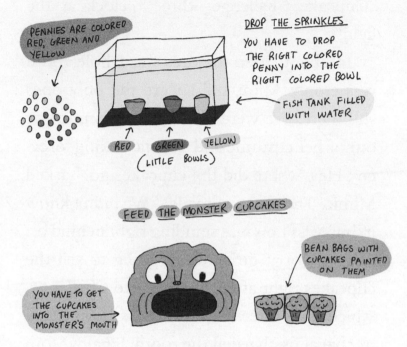

PENNIES ARE COLORED RED, GREEN AND YELLOW

DROP THE SPRINKLES
YOU HAVE TO DROP THE RIGHT COLORED PENNY INTO THE RIGHT COLORED BOWL

FISH TANK FILLED WITH WATER

RED   GREEN   YELLOW
(LITTLE BOWLS)

FEED THE MONSTER CUPCAKES

BEAN BAGS WITH CUPCAKES PAINTED ON THEM

YOU HAVE TO GET THE CUPCAKES INTO THE MONSTER'S MOUTH

Now that we had seen all the games in the room, I couldn't wait to get out and see the rest of the fair. Mom was going to walk around with Mimi and me, and she promised that we could have both cotton candy and popcorn. "Don't forget!" shouted Miss Lois. "Cupcake Challenge—three o'clock at the field!"

In about three minutes the whole room was empty. Mimi and I were the only ones still there. We were waiting for Mom to get out of her costume and she was taking forever. "Hey, where did the cupcakes go?" asked Mimi. "The ones we made?" We didn't know it, but Miss Lois was standing right behind us. "Don't worry, girls. We're going to sell the cupcakes right after the Cupcake Challenge, which is at three o'clock." Miss Lois tipped her hat at us, then left the room. Finally, Mom showed up.

"That costume was a lot harder to take off than to put on," she complained. "Plus, you wouldn't believe how hot it was in there." She waved her hand in front of face. Her face was red and her hair was messed up, but I didn't say anything because I wanted to get out to the giant slide, not wait another ten minutes while she fixed herself up in the bathroom. "Can we go?" I asked. Mom sighed and said, "Okay, but if you see a drinking fountain let me know."

THE SCHOOL FAIR

The school fair is pretty much the same every year, so we knew exactly where everything was. After the giant slide we got a hot dog, popcorn, and cotton candy, and then we played some of the regular games. If you win enough tickets, you can pick out a prize at the prize booth. Mimi and I got the same prize, except her bracelet was red and mine was blue.

BRACELETS

By two-thirty, both Mimi and I were ready for the Cupcake Challenge to start. It was too early to go to the field, so we went on the giant slide two more times to use up time.

THE CUPCAKE CHALLENGE

At ten to three, it was finally time to go. Everyone was there, and everyone was excited. I could see stuff set up over to the left, but it was hard to tell what we were going to have to do.

Last year for the Bird Challenge, people had to wear flippers and walk like a duck. It was really funny to watch, but I was pretty sure we weren't going to do that this year. Flippers don't have anything to do with cupcakes.

Mr. Clausen, the gym teacher, and Miss Lois were on the field. Mr. Clausen shouted through his megaphone, "PLEASE STAND WITH YOUR TEAM." Everyone says that

Mr. Clausen used to be in the army. I believe it, because he is a person who likes to yell. He's nice, but he's kind of scary too.

When everyone was together he said, "WELCOME TO THE CUPCAKE CHALLENGE! LINE UP IN A ROW WITH YOUR TEAM BEHIND THE WHITE LINE." Usually whenever our class has to do something unusual there is lots of talking, but this didn't happen today. Everyone was probably like me—not wanting to do anything wrong. Nobody wants to get yelled at by a person holding a megaphone. Even Robert Walters and Owen 1 lined up perfectly. "I want to go first," whispered Ruth. I think all of us were glad about that. No one complained.

Mr. Clausen looked around to make sure everyone was doing the right thing, and then he explained how the challenge was going to work.

While I was listening I looked around. Only four of the teams that were lined up were not from our class. I guess the Cupcake Challenge wasn't as popular if you weren't in Miss Lois's class. That was good for us. Less competition. Suddenly I was feeling like my team had a chance to win.

Mr. Clausen held the megaphone for Miss Lois and she said, "NOW REMEMBER, THIS IS JUST FOR FUN." She was trying to make us not nervous, but it didn't help. We were too nervous and too excited for a sentence to change anything. I put the words together in my head.

NERVOUS + EXCITED = NERCITED

I looked over at Mimi. She gave me a thumbs-up and smiled. That was different: that helped, a little bit.

THE RACE

As soon as the whistle blew, Ruth was gone. Suddenly I wasn't nervous anymore—just excited. She's a fast runner. That was a surprise. I didn't know she could run so fast. When she got to the far white line she put on a chef's hat, grabbed a flour bag, opened it up, and emptied the flour into a bowl. Suddenly there was dust everywhere. It was hard to see her behind the cloud.

The parent volunteer said something to her and pointed to the ground. Ruth picked up a wooden spoon and stuck it in the middle of the bowl. It was good that there were parent helpers on the other side telling us what to do. I never would have remembered all that stuff. When Ruth had everything perfect like she was supposed to, the parent volunteer pointed to us and Ruth came running back to our white line holding the bowl. Some of the other teams dropped their spoons, but she didn't. She was amazing. We were in first place!

Robert Walters was next. When he got to the far white line, he put on an apron and then had to open an egg carton and take out an egg. He picked up a spoon and put the egg on the spoon to carry it. He was supposed to run back all the way with the egg on the spoon, but that was pretty impossible to do. The egg kept falling off. It's a good thing they were hard-boiled eggs, or we would have all been in big trouble. I was shouting so much, my throat hurt. But I didn't care—I was excited and I was next.

As soon as Robert Walters tagged my hand, I ran. I was running next to Sandra Orr. I tried extra hard to beat her. It felt good to get to the white line one step before she did.

WHAT WAS NOT EASY

As soon as I got there the helper mom said, "Put one cupcake liner in each space in the muffin tin. And when you're done with that, pick it up with the oven mitts." It wasn't easy to get the cupcake liners into the muffin tin. They all wanted to stick together. After I got the last one in, I put on the oven mitts and picked up the tin.

MUFFIN TIN WITH HOLES IN IT.

CUPCAKE LINER.

YOU HAVE TO PUT ONE IN EACH HOLE.

WHAT WAS IMPOSSIBLE

Running with the muffin tin. All the muffin liners kept blowing out. It was impossible to keep them in the tin. Finally I just had to walk really fast instead of running. Holding the muffin tin up straight with the oven mitts wasn't easy either. I don't know if my part of the relay looked hard or not, but it was.

WHAT WAS A RELIEF

To be done. "Good job," said Ruth. I was going to say thank you, but she had already turned around and was yelling at Owen 1.

"GO, OWEN!" she yelled. Owen 1 had the hardest part. He had to put on a fake mustache and then carry a tall, fancy tray with three little balls on it in one hand and have a napkin draped over his other arm. It's good that they put the balls in cupcake liners; otherwise it would have been impossible, but still it looked really hard.

THE BALLS ON THE TRAY.

HIS FUNNY MUSTACHE.

THE NAPKIN OVER HIS ARM.

THIS IS NOT EASY.

I bet this race was really fun to watch if you weren't in it and trying to win it. I thought Owen 1 was doing a pretty good job, until I looked over and saw that Max and Brian Aber were almost at the finish line. "Go, Owen 1!

RUN!" I couldn't help it. I had to shout. Even though Owen 1 wasn't going to win, we shouted for him all the way. "That was awesome!" shouted Robert Walters. Without thinking I yelled, "Yeah!" and high-fived him.

"Did we win?" asked Owen 1. We all shook our heads. I thought he was going to be upset, but he said, "That was fun. I wish we could do it again." He wasn't the only one feeling that way. That was the exact same feeling I was having too.

WHAT IS AMAZING

Mimi's team won. Even though my team didn't even come close to winning, none of us could stop smiling. I looked around for Mom and saw her standing over in the cupcake line. I had completely forgotten that my cupcakes were for sale. Suddenly I had an idea.

While everyone was crowding around Miss Lois and Mr. Clausen, I ran over to Mom. "Oh, I was just going to buy you a cupcake," said Mom. "You did great. It was so much fun to watch." "Can you buy me eight?" I asked. Mom looked at me like I was crazy. "You're not going to eat eight cupcakes," she said. I patted my stomach and said, "But I'm soooo hungry." Mom didn't get my joke. "Mom! They're not all for me," I said. "I want to give them to my friends." "That's a lot of friends," said Mom. "Are you sure they all deserve one?" "Definitely!" I said. "And I want you to buy the cupcakes I made." Mom sighed and made me stand beside her so I could help carry them.

WHAT IS A LITTLE STRANGE

Buying your own cupcakes. Even though I made them, I still had to pay to get them.

CUPCAKES THINKING THEY BELONG TO ME

WHAT IS FUN

Watching people take a bite of something that you know they are going to love. "This is amazing," said Ruth. Robert Walters nodded. Even though he didn't say anything, I could tell that he loved it too. Owen 1 was in the bathroom, so I couldn't give him his yet. I ate my cupcake while I watched Miss Lois make the announcement about the winning team. It was exciting to see Mimi, Sammy, Max, and Sunni standing up in front of everybody. Mimi and Sunni put on the crowns Miss Lois had made, but Sammy and Max just held them. I looked at Miss Lois to see if she was upset about that, but she didn't seem to care.

After she took their photo, I gave them their cupcakes. Of course they loved them!

I was kind of hoping I could get Mom to buy me another cupcake, but when I went over to the cupcake table to look for her, I saw that all my cupcakes were gone. When something is a good thing, people find out about it fast. There were other cupcakes there, but I didn't want one of those. Once your tongue has tasted amazing, it can't go back to regular.

WHAT IS NOT EASY

To hold a delicious cupcake and not eat it.

DON'T EAT OWEN 1'S CUPCAKE.
DON'T EAT OWEN 1'S CUPCAKE.

ME USING ALL MY ENERGY → TO FIGHT AGAINST THE POWER OF THE DELICIOUS CUPCAKE

EAT ME!

A HUGE SURPRISE

When Owen 1 came back from the bathroom, he handed me a card. Even though he made a big excuse about it, it was still really nice. My whole team had signed it.

HERE, MY MOM MADE ME MAKE IT BECAUSE YOU LET US DO THE PROJECT AT YOUR HOUSE AND WE USED ALL YOUR STUFF.

OWEN 1 BEING UNCOMFORTABLE

THE CARD

"He kind of wrecked it," said Ruth, and she pointed to the front of the card. "That wasn't my fault!" complained Owen 1. "Both you and Robert were talking to me at the same time and telling me different things to write." "I said to write *fun*," said Robert. "And

I said to write *nice*," said Ruth. "Nobody said *fice*," said Robert.

THANK You
FOR BEING
FICE

← THE FRONT
OF THE CARD.

I looked over at Owen 1. He was getting mad. His face was scrunched up. He was about to say something that was going to wreck the moment and make everybody upset. I could tell.

"Here!" I said. I shoved his cupcake into his hand. For a second he was confused. His brain was probably deciding which to do: say what he was going to say, or eat the cupcake. A cupcake is a hard thing to ignore, especially if it is in your hand. Owen 1 took a huge bite.

I smiled. "I like *fice!*" I said. "It's perfect." And the funny thing is I was 100 percent telling the truth.

FUN + NICE = FICE

Owen 1 just nodded and chewed. He couldn't say a thing. Not with Grandma's perfect cupcake in his mouth. And even though Grandma was all the way in France, she'd done what she thought she couldn't do—help me at the fair.

WHAT HAPPENED AFTER THAT

Mom said I could walk home with Mimi, Sammy, and Max. As soon as we started walking, both Sammy and Max put their crowns on. When we got to my house, they ordered me to make more cupcakes. "You're not the kings of me," I said, but secretly I was thinking like them. More cupcakes sounded like a good idea.

After they left, Mimi and I went inside, and there right on the table by the door was a postcard from Grandma. It was a picture of the Eiffel Tower.

"I wish I could go there," I said. "Me too," said Mimi. "Let's go one day together," said Mimi. It was a great idea. Mimi and me on top of the Eiffel Tower. That would be perfect! "Pinky swear?" I asked. Mimi looked at me for a second, and then held out her pinky. It was a pinky swear I was 100 percent sure I would never break.

AMAZING

"France is amazing!" I said. "I know something more amazing than France," said Mimi. I looked at her and shrugged. "What?" I asked. "That you're friends with Owen 1," said Mimi, and she laughed. "We're not friends," I said. "It's something different." But she was sort of right. Now Owen 1 wasn't only just annoying. Now he was sometimes okay.

ANNOYING + OKAY = ANNOKAY

Nothing cures shock like sharing a surprise cupcake, even if it is kind of squished.

And I found another superpower that the guessing ball doesn't know about.

CUPCAKE RECIPE

CHOCOLATE CUPCAKES

Makes 16 standard cupcakes or 12 standard and 12 mini cupcakes

1 ¾ cups all-purpose flour

¼ cup unsweetened cocoa powder

¾ teaspoon baking soda

½ teaspoon baking powder

½ teaspoon salt

1 ½ sticks (12 tablespoons) unsalted
   butter, softened

¾ cup lightly packed brown sugar

2 large eggs

2 ounces unsweetened chocolate, melted

1 cup buttermilk

1 teaspoon vanilla extract

1. Preheat the oven to 350°F. Line the muffin cups with paper liners.

2. Whisk together the flour, cocoa powder, baking soda, baking powder, and salt in a medium bowl. In another medium bowl, with an electric mixer on high, beat the butter and sugar until light and fluffy, about 3 minutes.

3. Add the eggs, one at a time, beating well after each addition. Beat in the melted chocolate. Reduce the speed to low and add the flour mixture alternately with the buttermilk in batches, beginning and ending with the flour mixture and beating just until blended. Stir in the vanilla.

4. Spoon half of the batter into a ziplock bag. Snip a ¼-inch corner from the bag and fill

the paper liners two-thirds full. Repeat with the remaining batter. Bake until golden and a toothpick inserted in the center comes out clean, 15 to 20 minutes. Remove the cupcakes from the baking pan, place on a wire rack, and allow to cool completely.

FROSTING RECIPE

ALMOST-HOMEMADE VANILLA BUTTERCREAM
Makes 3 ½ cups

1 container (16 ounces) Marshmallow Fluff
3 sticks (¾ pound) unsalted butter,
    softened and cut into 1-inch pieces

VANILLA

BUTTER

1 teaspoon vanilla extract

½ cup confectioners' sugar, plus

additional sugar if necessary

SUGAR

Spoon the Marshmallow Fluff into a large bowl. Beat with an electric mixer on low. Gradually add the butter pieces, beating well after each addition, until smooth. Add the vanilla extract and the ½ cup confectioners' sugar. Scrape the bowl well to incorporate. Add more confectioners' sugar, if necessary, to adjust the texture.

WE FEEL SO FANCY.

WHAT GRACE WILL BE THINKING ABOUT IN HER NEXT BOOK